Arslan Khasavov, a Kumyk by nationality born in 1988, spent his childhood in Turkmenistan. He graduated from Asia and Africa Institute in Moscow in 2010 and spent a year at Damask University. He also took a degree from the Moscow Literary Institute. In 2008, his novel *Sense,* nominated for the Debut Prize, merited a special commendation of the jury, and in 2009 his short story collection *One More Chance for Glory* was again singled out by the Debut jury. The same year the book was a finalist of the "Faculty" Prize and the Astafyev Prize. His next novel: *Paradise under the Shade of Swords*, describes an ordinary country boy who is gradually drawn into a Jihad war.

Arslan contributes to major periodicals and also writes columns on the Northern Caucasus for the BBC Russian Service.

His work first appeared in English in the 2010 Glas anthology *Squaring the Circle* which toured the UK and US in 2011.

GLAS NEW RUSSIAN WRITING

contemporary Russian literature

in English translation

Volume 54

This is the 4th volume in the Glas sub-series of young Russian authors, winners and finalists of the Debut Prize created by the Pokolenie Foundation for humanitarian projects. Glas acknowledges its generous support in publishing this book.

Arslan Khasavov
SENSE

a novel

Translated by Arch Tait

GLAS Publishers
tel./fax: +7(495)441-9157
perova@glas.msk.su
www.glas.msk.su

USA and CANADA
Consortium Book Sales and Distribution
1094 Flex Drive
Jackson, TN 38301-5070
tel: 800-283-3572; fax: 800-351-5073
orderentry@perseusbooks.com

In the UK
CENTRAL BOOKS
orders@centralbooks.com
www.centralbooks.com
Direct orders: INPRESS
Tel: 0191 2308194
customerservices@inpressbooks.co.uk
www.inpressbooks.co.uk

Within Russia
Jupiter-Impex
www.jupiterbooks.ru

Editors: Natasha Perova & Joanne Turnbull
Design by Tatiana Shaposhnikova
Front cover picture courtesy of Sever Publishing House

ISBN 978-5-7172-0093-6

Dedicated to those not afraid to dissent

We talk to ourselves, oblivious to the surprised looks of those around us. We come into the world to live, but are constantly dying, sometimes to be reborn. In decrepit, evil-smelling hospitals where patients are compelled to swab toilet floors, at prestigious universities where the individuality you came with is taken from you. We come to travel the circle line of the Metro, lulled to sleep, our heads lolling, and many never get out of the carriage. We come to watch the lives of others in cinemas, lives full of adventures which will never happen to us, lives of people we shall never know because they do not exist. We come to drink tea with our family, remembering it as our happiest moment when it is no longer possible. We come to yawn at the memory of a family member we really, truly loved. We come into the world to run frantically throughout our lives in pursuit of success which throughout our lives taunts us from the other side of the river. And we always find something to console us as we live under the microscope of the One whose idea all this was in the first place.

Artur Kara

Majorities have never been really right, only minorities.

Pier Paolo Pasolini

What should we do? Smash everything properly, once and for all, and take the suffering on ourselves! What? Don't you understand? You will... Freedom and power, but first and foremost, power! Over all of cowering creation, over the whole ant heap! That's the goal! Remember that!

Fyodor Dostoevsky

During the French Revolution both religious institutions and the whole system of government were thrown into the melting pot, with the result that men's minds were in a state of utter confusion; they knew neither what to hold on to, nor where to stop. Revolutionaries of a hitherto unknown breed ... men who carried audacity to the point of sheer insanity; who baulked at nothing and, unchecked by any scruples, acted with an unprecedented ruthlessness. Nor were these strange beings mere ephemera, born of a brief crisis and destined to pass away when it ended. They were, rather, the first of a new race of men who subsequently made good and proliferated in all parts of the civilized world, everywhere retaining the same characteristics. We found them at the moment of their appearance in the world and they are still before our eyes.

Alexis de Tocqueville

Viscous Lenin descends like a mist
On cabin door handles on the seven seas;

Rusty Marx gnaws through ribbing and bracing
of metal-making plant administration;

Black Nietzsche crawls crab-like from the ruin;
And swollen as a baobab emerges Buddha;

And sharp Limonov like the thorn of prickly bush
In a Ukraine of airborne ghosts,
In a Ukraine of dreams and Gogol and elms,
Of beeches, oaks and groves as camps...

Such are we. But what of you?
We're unworldly, you are of the world.

Eduard Limonov

Majorities have never been really right, only minorities.

Pier Paolo Pasolini

What should we do? Smash everything properly, once and for all, and take the suffering on ourselves! What? Don't you understand? You will... Freedom and power, but first and foremost, power! Over all of cowering creation, over the whole ant heap! That's the goal! Remember that!

Fyodor Dostoevsky

During the French Revolution both religious institutions and the whole system of government were thrown into the melting pot, with the result that men's minds were in a state of utter confusion; they knew neither what to hold on to, nor where to stop. Revolutionaries of a hitherto unknown breed ... men who carried audacity to the point of sheer insanity; who baulked at nothing and, unchecked by any scruples, acted with an unprecedented ruthlessness. Nor were these strange beings mere ephemera, born of a brief crisis and destined to pass away when it ended. They were, rather, the first of a new race of men who subsequently made good and proliferated in all parts of the civilized world, everywhere retaining the same characteristics. We found them at the moment of their appearance in the world and they are still before our eyes.

Alexis de Tocqueville

Viscous Lenin descends like a mist
On cabin door handles on the seven seas;

Rusty Marx gnaws through ribbing and bracing
of metal-making plant administration;

Black Nietzsche crawls crab-like from the ruin;
And swollen as a baobab emerges Buddha;

And sharp Limonov like the thorn of prickly bush
In a Ukraine of airborne ghosts,
In a Ukraine of dreams and Gogol and elms,
Of beeches, oaks and groves as camps...

Such are we. But what of you?
We're unworldly, you are of the world.

Eduard Limonov

1

I often dream of my pages running through fingers like water; of my clever, exquisite words penetrating the minds of lovable creatures – girls in the Metro, pensive boys on lonely beds. I imagine a day when, among the thousands of books in bookshops and libraries, I will find the spine of mine – look, there's my name, the title of my book. I'll open it, pausing between the shelves, and start to browse, and be delighted with myself, and find life good, and the world incredibly rewarding. When I weary of turning the pages, I will return the book to its place and retire to the sidelines, out of everyone's way, as if not really there at all, just my observant spirit looking at my creation from a distance, looking to see who it is going to attract. Even if in an entire day my book is touched only by the warm hand of a connoisseur, I will exult. With tears of joy I will run to hug this person who has such excellent taste and tell him, yes, that is my book. I am the author. Amazed, he will turn to gaze admiringly at me. What a personality, the possessor of that gaze will think. This is the face of one blessed by fortune. For a moment we will be like brothers who have found each other after long, absurd years of being parted. I will seize the volume in one hand and with the other lead my reader to the payment desk. I will talk incessantly as tears stream down my face. Self-conscious, I will dab them away with a carefully ironed handkerchief. What a personality – so well groomed and the writer of brilliant books! I will buy the book, pay every last ruble and present it to him. I will upbraid the shop assistant. Bring more copies from the store! Can't you see how my creation is flying off the shelves, you blind chicken? What a personality! Ooh, ever so sorry, I'll attend to it right away.

A few years will pass and I will have developed a paunch. By now there will be more volumes bearing my name on the world's bookshelves and I will no longer be quite as refined and elegant as in the previous paragraph. I won't give a toss about my reader, just as long as he keeps buying my books. If he does, I will love him, and if he doesn't, I will tighten my belt.

Translators will slave over my writings. What a personality! I have tried translating a few things myself, and know from experience that a translator is the most attentive reader. He has to transfer an author's thoughts from one language into another. No problem if you know both languages well, you might think, but actually you need also to be smart, not just to have a wide vocabulary. What sounds fine and clearly expresses an idea in one language can, if translated literally, lose its flavour and perhaps even cease to make sense. Your translator has to find a solution.

I tried translating a novel myself, Charles Bukowski's *Ham on Rye*, and sweated over how to convey the concept of a Model-T in Russian. Suppose Bukowski writes, "We got into the Model-T and drove over to see my Grandfather Leonard". I translated that literally into Russian. But how many people in Russia know what a Model-T is? Obviously it's a mode of transport, but the picture is marred. I diligently headed to the Historical Library, found the book in Russian and looked to see how a professional translator got round the problem. He translated it, "We got into the Ford and drove over to see my Grandfather Leonard". Tricks of the trade. You are thinking, "What a personality! He even translates and looks stuff up in libraries."

So what's stopping me from writing? Not any lack of imagination, as you will already have gathered, and in any case, reality gives plenty of help, propelling you towards fantasy. At night, with the blinds closed so tightly you can't see the moon or the sky or the lights outside, I gaze at the ceiling. It is serene. Oh, ceiling mine, would that I had your serenity! Would that I had your imperturbability, ceiling mine! Light-bulbs smile down. Suddenly, coruscating lines of prose light up above me, white, three-dimensional, brilliant. They whizz near and even through me and disappear as suddenly as they appear. I jump up, grab a pillow and beat them. The pillow passes straight through, the light sparkles, but the games it plays oppress me. The walls are closing in. There is no escape. I try to read and take in the meaning of these messages but they are too bright. I shut my eyes. Failing to make out a single word, I fall back on the bed and close my eyes in search of peace. I know a technique for getting an idea out of your mind. Just lie down, shut your eyes and think about something else: a really good day you've enjoyed, the best you can think of. Totally immerse yourself in it and, when you re-surface, you'll find the idea you were trying to get rid of has gone away. I call this self-distraction and I am a great writer, so you should call it that too unless you come up with something more original. The light seeps through my eyelids. My eyelashes flutter in the wind that brings these letters to me from the world beyond. (I have very long eyelashes. Everybody notices.)

No, it is impossible to concentrate under these circumstances! I need to self-distract. Pushing my head under the pillow, I sniff my own odour. Yes, my smell. Like a moment of insight that idea hits me. What is my scent like? Do I smell good or bad? Is it attractive or repellent? Do people like it or turn up their noses in disgust? Why can't I usually smell it? Why does it nestle beneath a mantle of other smells, overlaid by their laboured exhalations? It is, after all, my nearest and dearest smell. I should always smell it, whether in moments of joy or adversity, but here it is coyly hiding under the pillow. It really is the most unusual smell in all the world. If you go into a perfume shop, walk past the display cases with a consultant (or without), spray some perfume on a slip of cardboard, inhale one new product, another, then perhaps a delicate classic, you know straight away. Either you like it or you don't. Of course, a perfume can be neither one thing nor the other, producing no reaction positive or negative. It can be unmemorable. It may have something, there is something you sense, but it evanesces without plucking at a heartstring, so to speak. Here, however, I detect my own scent and that is a different matter! How devious it is! It dissipates, seeking to elude me. I stick my nose in the sheet and inhale deeply. No, almost nothing. The pitiful relict of the scent of a great man and major writer.

To a museum with it, this sheet! To a museum. At once! Eager crowds want, if not to sniff it (in a museum it will only smell of time), then at least to glimpse it. A boy will place his hand on the glass case even as attendants shout, "Don't lean on the glass!" The destiny of my sheet will unfold in strict accordance with how successful I am in the struggle for immortality. If my, as yet uncelebrated, name is destined for oblivion, its fate will be lamentable. It will serve out its days as a duster. If instead my fame grows and holds sway through the centuries over the minds of readers of an as yet indiscernible future, it will be tended and pampered. Museum experts specializing in exhibits made of cotton will restore it and keep it from deteriorating.

How strange that an object's history should be made by the person who used it, quite without its active participation. Here I am, lying on it right now, sheltered from the glittering lines of my revelation, breathing in my own evanescent scent and dreaming of undying glory and what will have become of my bedsheet a hundred years from now. Will my fame survive that long? Oh, sheet, your isolation is no less than that of man, no less total is the unknown which surrounds you, even if you aren't the least bothered by that. I press myself to the sheet in an access of intimacy and whisper to it, "We all aspire to immortality, but for most of us it is beyond reach." Shedding a redemptive tear, I fall asleep.

2

When I woke the following afternoon, I saw with total clarity that no book I might ever write, no insight of genius (there are already so many of both out there that you will never assimilate them all) could bring me the fame I might gain by direct intervention in the smooth flow of history. Although art is assuredly a part of history, history trumps it a hundred times over. The movies of the 1920s and 1930s which, it was believed, would stand the test of time are now known only to a handful of cinema critics and their ilk. Outstanding books of the 1940s are lucky to be reprinted nowadays in an edition of 500 copies, while theatre productions of the past get even shorter shrift from the general public. These are examples from the last century, and for people today the more distant past is even more obscure and wearisome. There are Shakespeare with his banal tales, Cervantes (original style, admittedly), and the nineteenth-century classics of Russian literature which we studied on the principle: "what you can't do, we teach you; what you won't do, we make you". There are exceptions, let us never forget the ubiquitous 'but', – but let us also face the fact that, sooner or later works of art become obsolete. That is sad but true of art, but not of history. History can be rewritten to suit a government but it can never be changed. Ultimately it is up to every independently-minded person to decide for themselves what, in a particular series of historical events, was good and what was evil. Art is a representation of history, literal or distorted, while the instant I typed that proposition into my computer is already history.

I, an indubitably great, if as yet undiscovered, writer, need to make the world sit up. But how do I get everyone talking about me and arguing about my personality? The problem is that here I am, reclining meditatively in a room with blinds which block out the light, and not even most of the neighbours know my name.

I suddenly saw what was needed! Only a revolution would produce the requisite outcome. A sudden change of regime, anywhere in the world, but under my leadership. Proclamation of myself as ruler, popular acclaim. I pictured it vividly.

Greatly excited, I leapt on to the smooth laminate of the floor and in an instant stood before my map of the world. Here, maybe, or here, or ...?

Starting with Russia, I began analyzing the feasibility of forcible regime change. No, in one place it wouldn't work, in another it wasn't needed. Not needed ... the most vital ideas always pop up unexpectedly. It hadn't occurred to me that this was an endeavour which couldn't be accomplished by one man acting alone, no matter how great. It had to be a mass movement, and I and the others in it would have to be fully committed to the idea that change was essential.

That ruled out Russia. As I ran my eye over all the countries of Eurasia, Africa, America, Australia and even Antarctica, I lapsed into reverie. Antarctica. Does it actually belong to anyone? I saw myself, backed by hundreds of thousands of dolphins, seals and other sea creatures, advancing on the enemy. From the air, birds attacked, dropping rocks on their ranks and squirting copious amounts of guano down on them. 'Queen Maud Land', 'Wilkes Land', 'Ellsworth Land' and even smaller territories. Imagine how surprised Queen Maud, Wilkes and Ellsworth would be by the appearance of a great writer in their lands, and one backed, moreover, by such a mighty force.

"LOL, pal!" I berated myself. "Antarctica? What use is Antarctica to you? You'll die of cold and hunger there before you win glory and fame. The conqueror of Antarctica? Dunderhead! Half-wit! Fantasist! Albeit, a great one," I conceded to make myself feel better. I lay down on my leather rug with its fur inserts and put my hands behind my head. The iron light fitting dangled menacingly above me. I closed my eyes and pictured the impending battles. First I would write the book that was in me. It would be quite something. I would hide it in a remote place known only to myself and with an unwavering hand instruct in my Will, "Greatly esteemed father and mother, no matter where I make the supreme sacrifice, no matter what banners I have fought under, beyond good and evil (or not), know now that the last wish of your only son is that his work should be published. You will find it at ..." My parents would hasten to that location and retrieve a package containing the manuscript. It would provide comfortably for their old age and proclaim to the world that the hero who fought so ruthlessly on the stage of history had yet a sensitive, vulnerable soul; and formidable writing talent.

"It matters not what lands you conquer, nor yet how victorious your campaign! The main thing is to resolve to die young, if that be ordained, not flinching should death look into your eyes. With the spear, assure your place, a page or a paragraph, in the history books." Damn, I still don't have a portrait. Must put that right. Work on the look.

Remember Rasputin's eyes? How long you gazed into that hypnotic stare, how long you practised in front of the mirror. The next day people did sit up and pay attention in the bus. Or did you imagine that, Artur Kara? You are such a fantasist! So what?! Do you see your address to the people, live on all TV channels? The streets are deserted, cars as rare as men in the desert. Everybody is glued to their televisions, waiting to hear what you will say, straining to catch your every word, all admiring you. Kara is great! How handsome he is! What a personality! Or you are on your deathbed, a grievous wound visible on your body but your face as unblemished as a baby's. "God has been kind to him," someone will say, and I will expire, fulfilled.

For me death has never been something to fear. It is a fact of life. You have life, and when it ends you are dead. What matters is not that death comes to you but how you accept it. I shall not falter. I shall not seek to be spared the scythe. I am sure of myself.

But to pull off something as classy as that you need not only intellectual power, but brute physical strength. Asian martial arts, massive, pumped-up muscles, robust lungs. Who knows what may have to be faced? The guys in power there are going to be no pushover. They have an army, they have security, weapons, and they have the law fighting on their side. They have prisons. They have money. They have a lot. Against them, what have I got? I've got me. I've got the fingers typing this text and a keyboard to wind them up with symbolism, a mosaic of letters which gives life to thoughts they haven't foreseen. And that's about all I do have. Even death is not on my side but somewhere in between, watchful, ready to take a bite out of our flank or theirs.

My thoughts carried me far away. Rising above the floor, I spread my arms wide, while keeping my feet together. Disregarding the laws of gravity, ignoring Newton and his apple, I hovered between the leather and fur rug and the metal light fitting. Relaxing my concentration, I fell back to the floor, rolled over on to my stomach and started furiously doing press-ups. I needed strength, brute physical strength but my muscles were embryonic. I managed fifteen press-ups before getting up, out of breath. I started working out with dumbbells. When I had a good feeling about my arms, I turned my attention to my abs. Hell! If not totally neglected, they were certainly in need of urgent attention. Getting back down on the floor and locking my toes under the wardrobe, I started feverishly doing sit-ups but had barely managed five when Djennet, my mum, came in.

"How many times do I have to tell you to desist from this plebeian habit of coming in without knocking! We are not in a lift, so don't just wander in as if it's the most natural thing in the world! I might be in the middle of writing a secret plan to build a just society which will transform social relations throughout the entire world, and you just come barging in." Getting to my feet, I loosened myself with a good shake.

"I need you to take the rubbish out." It's always the same. No sooner are you imagining you are God knows who, taking off into sublime realms, as far as your imagination can carry you, than someone bursts into the world of your dreams without knocking and wrecks everything with their crassness. "Okay."

There was too much rubbish in the sack and I had to squash it before it would fit into the opening of the rubbish chute. As I did so, I thought of the fame and glory which awaited me. "Well, so what?" I consoled myself. "What's so humiliating about taking out the rubbish. It's just a chore. Somebody has to do it. And sweeping the streets is something somebody has to do too," I suddenly raged, "but it's not you, not Kara the Great, mighty man of valour, who ought to be doing it." I pulled the squashed bag of rubbish back out of the opening and took it back to our apartment.

"Never, do you hear me, never ask me to do anything like that again!" I yelled as I came in the door. "You have no idea of the stature of the person with whom you co-exist, you sad, ordinary person! You just don't know with whom you are talking!" My disdain was palpable. "You are wholly unaware of how privileged you are!"

My startled mother ran over and stared at my countenance in disbelief. "Artur, dear, are you all right?" She ran her hand first through my hair then over my cheek. Oh, dear God, how warm and tender was the touch of my mother's hand! And I, the lowliest of men, had dared to raise my voice to her, the mother who had given me the opportunity to be part of life on this Earth! I wept. I flung the rubbish on the floor, took her hand and kissed it repeatedly. My mother, my own sweet mother, how long forgotten were these caresses, a reminiscence of childhood where there was no sorrow and it seemed that life would last forever, where my mother stroked me like this every day as she sat on the edge of my bed, and hundreds and thousands of times we vowed the tenderest love and eternal devotion to each other.

My tears started forth with new vigour, a downpour watering my mother's hand, falling on her fingers and flowing down, or dripping into her palm, to the life line and all those other lines. The tears distorted my world, blurring everything I could see, but in that morass I made out my mother's expression. She looked scared. Not a jot of pity, joy or love. No tears. Just fear. Animal fear.

The moment I discerned that reality, the unanticipated access of tenderness which had visited me vanished, evaporated into the air we were breathing. Her fear sucked in all my tenderness, swallowed it whole. Violently thrusting her hand away from my person, filled with resentment and hatred of everything and everyone on Earth, I set about her.

"You pathetic specimen! You have never understood me, don't you see? You, my mother, have never truly understood me! Never! Those few moments of spiritual intimacy were not with you! It was your soul sat with me then when I was a child! You understand nothing! You were afraid of me, you have always been afraid of me! Of my thoughts and actions!"

"Artur, you're sick," she pronounced.

I have to explain here to readers that my mother was incapable of understanding me. Shuffling off my sneakers, wiping the last of the wetness from my face, I proceeded to my room, my headquarters, shut the door behind me and turned the key. Falling back on the bed, I put my hands behind my head and started thinking through my plans. I needed to attract people to my cause. I had never liked people, the crowd, the masses, but I needed them. My mum might have no part to play in the struggle, but she was an ideal training facility. I must cast aside all emotion, all principle, and forget my memories. I must only advance towards my goal, dedicate myself to that. I am a man without a past. I am a man without a past. I am a man without a past. But I had no doubt about my future. It was going to be big and I would make it great. How could underlings appreciate what I had in mind? They were the masses, rabble.

What is it I find so distasteful about them? They are as alike as two drops of my salt tears, their lives a complete waste of time, their inner world vacuous. All they ever read is banalities. The unconventional holds no appeal for them. They call a possessed man an animal, and, seeing him on their TV screen, rant, "I'd give 'im what for, that shit! How come someone like that is even allowed to live in this country?" They rage, sensing danger, making no attempt to understand the grandeur of the stunts some possessed men get up to. They are blind to what is being protested about, they don't see his inner strength. Aware that they themselves would never be capable of anything of the sort, they affect to despise the possessed, but do talk about them. They warn you off them, but if they met one in the street they wouldn't dare lay a finger on him, let alone call him a shit to his face.

They value life above all else, unaware that a stupid life is without value. Their days are empty. In the morning they go off to a job which most of them don't like, and in the evening return exhausted to their den. Ask them why they work and they will nod towards their children and say, "Who else do you think is going to feed them?" The children they have nodded at will, with few exceptions, repeat their parents' history. They go to a pre-school nursery where they are taught to do what grown-ups tell them and be good. Then they go to a school where hardly any subject in the overloaded curriculum has the least practical value, and get a simple message dunned into their heads: do as your parents say and everything will be all right. They leave school thoroughly domesticated, and anything the carers at the nursery or the teachers at school have left undone will be tidied up by their colleagues in further education and the humiliation and beatings during conscription in the army. Any boisterous type who still hasn't been satisfactorily processed will sooner or later end up in jail for excessive attachment to the truth. Meanwhile, years pass.

Nothing can stop time's smooth flow. The smooth flow of time. You can stop the hands of a clock, smash and stamp on hundreds of them, but that will not stop time, and nobody will stop growing up or growing old while they are doing it. Time tranquillizes even the rowdiest. Most people released from prison just want to go straight and live a quiet life "like everybody else". "I want to learn to live among ordinary people," the ex-convict declares on TV. "Get a job, have a wife and kids ..." That's his goose cooked.

What else is there? People are victims. They need stability. They want to know at the very least that they are not going to die of hunger tomorrow, and preferably that in three, five or ten years' time they will be able to buy the car they can't afford today, to get their children into a good college, and redecorate their dilapidated apartment. Only 'normal' life can offer people that, only stultifying middle-class life. Life has never been stable for heroes. For them you're either at the top or you're nowhere. It's all or nothing, and you're likely to be invited to donate your life, like a coin you've been hoarding for a rainy day.

There doesn't seem to be anything new on offer, no different model for a life's work. Everything either harks back to the last century or holds no promise of quick, dramatic results. The worst of it is the sheer inanity of normal lives, the waste, the lack of anything to remember, the wistful summarizing at the end. "My life has passed in the blink of an eye! It seems only yesterday I was young, and tomorrow (God forbid!) I will die." Well, whose fault is that? Only your own, you stupid, gutless coward!

When I hear people going on like that, though, I just nod and murmur sympathetically, "That's life, isn't it? No wonder people say it flies by in the blink of an eye!" People do not like the truth and you have to throw them off the track. You have to at least pretend to be one of them, make it seem you're no more than their equal, and shove your greatness up your jumper for the time being. Everything will work out in the end. How could it not? You are a genius with the pen, a genius at living, and not afraid of dying. Ordinary people will be smitten and eventually put you up on the pedestal where you belong.

A feeling of serenity spread through my body, first filling my mind, then flowing down through veins, arteries and bones. It caressed my breast, diverted into my arms, doubled back to pour its milk into my stomach before moving down to my legs. I relaxed, sank into it.

Someone was tugging at the door handle, realized the door was locked, and knocked. (It's the only way you can teach them.)

"Artur," I heard my mother call. "Are you all right? I've brought you an aspirin. Do you want to take it?"

"No thanks, Mum! I feel a lot better. I'm really sorry!" I left a pause before adding, "I love you very much!"

"I love you too, son! I love you too!" I could hear from the quavering in her voice that she was touched.

"I'll just take a nap! I'll come out when I wake up. Don't worry about me! I really do feel better."

"That's good, son. I'm glad. Come out when you're ready." Retreating footsteps.

A chill ran over me and I crawled under the blanket. Everything was going according to plan. I had taken the first step on the road to success. So much harmony was making me drowsy. I turned on my side, face to the wall, and fell asleep.

3

I enjoy sleeping. In my sleep I often find a film adaptation of my hopes and dreams waiting for me. And here I am, standing at the podium in a spacious, brightly lit hall with a thousand red seats. There are handsome men in evening dress, beautiful ladies in sumptuous gowns. Black, red, white. Their bosoms heave in discreet décolleté. The men's eyes shine with admiration for the speaker, their palms sweat from emotion. The women give way to their feelings: here and there hankies are dabbed at eyes and embarrassed mirrors reflect smudged mascara. What a personality! Everybody is here just to see me.

An immense crystal chandelier in the centre of the ornate ceiling lights up already glowing faces and makes the jewels on necks and fingers and in ears sparkle. What a splendid evening, and all of it because of me! Thanks to me, but at the same time just for me! A large spotlight picks me out on the dark stage, me and the podium from which I am about to speak.

"Thank you, ladies and gentlemen, thank you! No, please, please! I want first of all to say thank you to my mother! Hi, Mum, hi!" (I wave into one of the many cameras.) "Yes, Mum, I did write that famous book. I said you would be proud of me one day! Thank you for giving me the opportunity to be alive and be a writer! Look at these people ..." (I see cameras turn on cue and start gliding over the audience.) "They are all grateful to you for your son, along with the millions of people who could not be fitted into this wonderful venue tonight..."

At this point my imagination adds a gold letter 'N' to the hitherto anonymous black lectern. (Oh, so that's what this is all about. I have been awarded the Nobel Prize.) At last my books have been appreciated! They have entries in encyclopedias and textbooks of Russian Literature. They are going to be studied at schools and universities. All that hard work has been to some purpose.

"Ah, you see, tears are welling up in my eyes. Forgive me this show of emotion. I am just a very sensitive soul, as you, my friends, having read my works, already know. What heroes I have populated them with, eh? Thank you, thank you! Yes, I have suffered, but I have reaped my reward. I wrote those works in a small room to the accompaniment of relaxing background music. Yes, friends, that room has now been made into a museum and you are all most welcome to visit it. Come, raise your cultural awareness and rub shoulders with the most talented people in the world, composers, writers, actors, artists. You yourselves are the best people in the world, and may be interested to know that with the million and a half dollars I have coming to me as the greatest writer in the universe I am planning to buy a really nice house. But needless to say, what I most value from this evening is the memories, the precious memories of this wonderful day. I thank you all!"

My audience burst into applause. They rise to their feet to demonstrate their adulation. I am speechless with emotion, feeling within me a great fullness of life at this moment, in this place. I am happy. I finally feel happy! When dreams come true, there are two possible outcomes: happiness or disillusionment, and I am happy, dammit! Not a twinge of disillusionment! Perhaps a tinge of sadness in this cocktail of jubilation, but only because the evening is drawing to a close and unlikely to be repeated.

"All good things come to an end," I console myself. "If you think about that too much you will only ever live at half throttle. You will fail to see the flashes of wondrousness because your eyes are shrouded by the pall of life's finitude. I'll hear no talk of an end. No talk of it. No talk. No end. Do you hear?!"

But the dream ends anyway. My imagination has nothing more to offer on this topic. What matters, though, what needs to be remembered is that only now am I calling this a dream. All that time, those seconds (minutes? hours?) I was experiencing everything in reality. For me, nothing was more real. That brightly lit hall, those handsome, wonderful people, the spotlight picking me out in the darkness ... even the emotion! Even the emotion choking my words was real.

When I opened my eyes, I was lying on my bed, but it wasn't that I found upsetting -- even geniuses are allowed to lie down sometimes – but that I was actually just a slob nodding off during the day rather than a brilliant Nobel Prize-winning writer. Never mind! My talent may as yet be unrecognized (I haven't yet written anything all that good), but think of my potential.

4

Entering the family room, I supplied the constituent missing from their entirety. Seated on three of the four chairs, they were dining. "You're awake. Come, sit down and have your dinner," my mother said, jumping up and beginning to fuss. My father gave me a stern and, I thought, disapproving look, while my sister pretended not to have noticed me.

Taking the vacant seat I turned to meet the disapproving look.

"Well now, Dad, how was your day?" I asked, giving him a pat on the shoulder and adding, "Tell us about it."

"Since when have you taken any interest in how my day was?" he parried with another, rather unfriendly, question.

I surveyed the contents of the plate before me. "Since when? I've always been interested. It's just that I kept forgetting to ask," I replied, tucking into the rice.

I decided it was time for me to deliver a short talk to them. "The fact is that we are a family," I said, looking, rather effectively I thought, into the eyes of each of them before turning to address my father directly. "Especially you and I. Father and son. Son and father. That's so important! Among the vicissitudes of everyday life we forget the meaning of those words. I quite understand. You have a job, I have my own interests, but we should be together, a force united. That applies to you women, too. We need to ..."

"I'm not a woman, I'm a young lady," my sister interrupted.

"A woman, a lady, a granny – what difference does it make? What matters is what blood flows in your veins and what family name you bear. We should not be disunited. We need to identify our common interests instead of pursuing the interests of each one of us in isolation. We should be one fist! One fist, d'you hear?"

"Have you gone bonkers?" my sister asked, articulating the sense of the meeting.

I heard my mother tell her husband sotto voce, "He hasn't been himself since yesterday."

"You probably want to know why I have become so concerned about this," I went on. Using hand gestures for greater impact, I began to explain. "I have had a revelation. Yes, a revelation. It happens, right?"

I did not read acquiescence in their faces. They appeared to suspect a practical joke in the situation and in my words. I had yet to command their trust.

I could understand that. It is always difficult to believe a person has suddenly changed. People do not change at the waving of a magic wand. Of course they don't. Someone was great yesterday, and today is suddenly only your equal. I too would find that difficult to believe. I had no time, however, to wait for them to gradually accept my new style, my new guise. I needed a mass following, and for a start I needed to enroll the people living under the same roof with me. I needed to create a single picture out of jigsaw pieces which had certain features in common.

On the other hand, your intimates are much more difficult to win round than people who don't know you. Henry Miller observed, rightly in my opinion, that those closest to you can in an instant become your main adversaries. Familiar with one aspect of you, they flatly refuse to believe you are capable of anything else. Let me instance an occasion when I, a great writer and, you will recall, future Nobel Prize winner, was talking to my parents about my progress as a man of letters only to be pulled up short by the question, "What bullshit have you been scribbling this time?" Clearly, considerable time would have to elapse for them to revise their judgment and, frankly, I didn't have time to spare.

"Well, can you really say I'm not right, Dad?"

"There's some truth in what you say, but let me ask you a question. Where have you been up till now? I wouldn't have mentioned it, but you've raised the matter."

"Islam, don't ..." Mum put her small hand over my father's veiny one.

"What do you mean, 'Don't'? How can I not? It's time this was said!" he rejected his wife's plea and turned to me. "It wouldn't matter so much if you just weren't interested in how we are doing. We are old and don't fit your ideal. The trouble is, though, that you don't care whether we are alive or dead. All right, I won't generalize. You don't care whether I am alive or dead! Whether I croak at that factory of mine trying to feed you and your sister! She at least has a head on her shoulders, but you ... all you know about is sticking your nose in a book and daydreaming. You haven't a penny to your name! If I go belly up tomorrow what will become of all of you? There's no way anyone can rely on you. You only think about yourself and you'd sooner run away from the family than think how to feed and clothe your sister, your mother, and maybe even give me some help. At your age I was raring to go, flogging my guts out, full of ambition!"

"He's ambitious too ..." Mum tried to intercede. My sister was showing no interest in this drama. Everything about her seemed to say, "It's obvious he's a loser. Why waste your breath?" Dad had really got the bit between his teeth, though, and the only person who could rein him in now was himself.

"Where's his ambition? What's he aiming to achieve? He lies about, he reads. Okay, I understand perfectly well that reading is a splendid thing, but when the family is barely making ends meet and someone with a good brain is lying around with a book in his hands, that I do find a bit difficult to understand. Tell me, Artur, what is your ambition? What do you want to get out of life? What do you want to achieve? Who do you want to be? That's something I really would be interested to know! Because in all my life I've never come across anyone like you, not in the army, not at the factory. Perhaps I belong in the last century and I'm far inferior to you, but just explain it to me. I'm well able to understand! You, Djennet, do you know what your son wants?" he asked, rounding on his wife.

"Let me give you your answer." I had always had my answer ready for this question, but hadn't expected I would ever have to give it. "I want to be ..." I was on the verge of giving away my secret, but came to my senses just in time. If I had told them, it would have been the end of everything! Raising a piala of green tea to my lips, I deftly substituted a serviceable answer and, after taking a sip, said, "I'll tell you what I want, what it is that impels me to continue this way of living which brings me neither joy nor satisfaction."

My father smiled quizzically. My mother feared some irrevocable rift, and my sister finally got round to staring at me. A large fly was buzzing at the kitchen window. Raindrops were tapping at it.

"What I want is your happiness. Don't laugh. Only stupid people laugh before they've heard what is being said. You complain that I'm only reading and don't have a penny to show for it. Yes, dammit, I am reading!" The energy welling up inside me shocked my body like a flash of lightning and was conducted to my head. Unable to contain the violence of the current, I leapt up from my chair, which catapulted backwards from the unexpectedness of my movement. Now on my feet and gesticulating dramatically, I continued, "Reading has never yet done anyone any harm, and anyway, do you know," I asked pointing at my father who was now listening to me, "or you, or perhaps you, smug airhead," I fired at my mother and sister respectively, "why I am doing this? For fun? Then let me ask you a question. What's stopping you from getting the same satisfaction? I'll tell you why I'm reading. I am stocking my mind. Do you know what that is? It is something that will make you all happy one day, and maybe me too! My knowledge will do something the hands of neither my father nor my mother can do. You have no idea what a joy it is to be in the company of the great! Remarque, Nietzsche, Kant, John Fante, Charles Bukowski – I would go on if I were talking to well-read people. When I'm in the company of the greats I can feel myself growing."

"What you are feeling is not what matters. What matters is that your family, your own children don't go hungry! He's stocking his mind, if you please! What good is having your mind stocked going to do anyone? This Nietzsche or Kant or those other two, whatever they're called, and your Mante and Zhukovsky ...." My Dad was in a right lather.

"Fante and Bukowski," I helped him out.

"That's not important," he went on. "Bukowski, Zhukovsky, Zhirinovsky, who cares? What good are they to you? They just take up your time and fill your head with a lot of nonsense! Your own special thoughts! Artur, I've told you more than once, you need to focus! You need to choose a direction which will lead you to success. You need to study every aspect of it, become a real expert, and then you will be a valuable member of society and we, – I, your mother, your sister, your future family – will be able to rely on you and trust you ... which we can't at present."

After delivering this homily, my father was motionless, lost in thought, his eyes unmoving. His semi-somnolent musing affected the whole room. Even the fly on the window cooled it and the rain outside slackened. I ran the fork over my plate, trying to discharge the tension. My father's empty stare was drilling a hole in my stomach. I was within an inch of waving my hand in front of his eyes to snap him out of it.

He unexpectedly started up again, but now more calmly. "Artur, you just have to understand that we your parents would never wish you harm. What parents would wish to see their child harmed? It's unthinkable." His voice was tired and there was sadness in his last words. "But of course it's up to you. I can't force you. It's your life. But, I beg you ..." The other two looked very surprised. It was the first time he had ever begged me for anything. "Yes, I beg you: please do as I say. Before it is too late! For the sake of all that's holy ... You will bitterly regret it if you don't take your chance. There is so much you could do! If I had been in your position there is so much I could have achieved. I just didn't have the opportunities. You know, I came from the countryside and my father, your grandfather, used to put a cross on documents because he couldn't even sign his name. I broke away from all that. I broke away from it in the hope that you, my son, would go on to greater things."

He stood up and went through to their bedroom. Stopping at the door, he fixed his eyes on me once more, said a barely audible "Good night", and retired. I imagine him unable to sleep for a long time, tormented by the metallic rattling of the rain. During the night a red rash developed on his right hand which soon spread to cover his whole body, leaving only his face clear. The doctors diagnosed eczema "resulting from emotional disturbance or excessive nervous tension".

After he left, I picked up the chair and headed for my room without saying another word. My sister stopped me in the hallway and hissed, "Who do you take after, freak?"

5

I can't say I was entirely unaffected by the failure with my family. I regretted, of course, that it turned out quite differently from what I had planned, but took it as a sign from above. It was a lesson that things are not always straightforward and that plans cannot always be implemented as you might wish.

"Never mind," I thought. "Nothing terrible has happened. Even if they failed to understand the genuineness of my ambitions, we did at least talk about important matters." Such things are not supposed to be discussed in our tradition. We ought to live in peace and we are not permitted to talk about emotions. We are supposed to co-exist in mutual respect with parents, to honour them, and not to talk to them as equals as I just had. That would be haraam, a sin. But we had talked like that and I was glad, because people often barely know their father and mother. They have a general idea of who they are, of course, but, without seeing into them more deeply, how can you know for sure? You end up baffled after they pass on, just as to this day we are baffled, wondering whether anyone will meet them up there or whether they will sink into a grim abyss of infinity.

Yes, I am a Muslim. I will put in a bit here for my biographers, right? You may in any case also be interested in the personality of the writer of these lines, where it came from and the circumstances under which it has developed.

I am a Kumyk. Not a Kulmyk or Kalmyk – a Kumyk. This once great nation had its own realm on its own plain. The country was called Kumykia and the plain, it may surprise you to learn, was known as the Plain of Kumykia. When I saw the light of day in the maternity ward of a hospital in Grozny, Chechnya, in 1987, lagging two years behind my sister, I instantly made a considerable impact. Not by the mere fact of my having appeared in this vale of tears. No, neither the doctor, the midwife, nor even my mother realized what a personality had just been born. They were not to know that the wrinkled little body cringing on the white sheets would one day become a great writer. Their amazement was over something quite different – my foot.

My foot was twisted, a deformity caused by a minor infection during pregnancy. The surgeons gave me two weeks in a special ward to get used to being in the world, and then they operated. The foot was straightened but evidence of the deformity remains with me to this day. The crepitus of bones offends delicate ears, and a circlet of scars right round my leg offends not only delicate eyes. A further invisible accompaniment of this mishap is pain. A constant ache made me cry as a child and later kept me from getting to sleep. I am used to it now, but it has haunted me since birth. Limping has become a habit which, unfortunately, I cannot break. I have to admit that even a well-stocked mind is of little avail.

Often, especially in the shower, I imagine I am a musical superstar performing in front of a packed stadium. The only props I need are a radio and a large mirror. I am happy in there, and I suffer. Sometimes I cry as I look into my own deep eyes. The mirror mists up but I soap it and it reflects my prolonged raptures. Some performers say they are only really alive on stage, but I say people are most alive in the shower. Taking a shower is such an intimate thing that it would be absurd to worry about society's prejudices. In the shower you can be anything you want. The absence of clothing is liberating. It lets you be natural and sometimes, if the occasion calls for it, a bit of an actor. I spend my time in there twisting and turning, excited, flying, and when I tire I sit down on the seat, contemplate the folds on my stomach, and think that some day that flab will dissolve and be replaced as if by magic by six-pack abs. In the shower you can contemplate anything without a twinge of conscience. The shower is a magic cubicle full of truth.

I need, however, to attain my goal. I, the great Artur Kara, am not one to rest content with hopeless dreams or be satisfied with the standing ovations which my imagination pours over me in the shower along with the streaming hot water. After our conversation, I pretty much knew where I stood with my family. Either they would never change their way of life (which seemed most likely) or they would change it only by a process of evolution, not instantly as I had hoped. I needed nevertheless to continue wearing my mask in order to get them used to it, habituated. But why had my sister not come over to my side? Why had she become the most implacable opponent of my transfiguration? She is only two years older than me. With adults one has to accept that their minds were formed by the environment they lived in when young, the circumstances of their lives and the events of which they were part. But my sister! Were there additional genetic constraints and personality traits needing to be taken into account here?

I am in urgent need of allies. I'm already twenty and need to get all this over and done with. After that I will be able to sit by the fire and mull over my past deeds – or lie on a prison bunk (perhaps the difference is not that great). Or die familiar with the salt taste of combat.

So what should I do today? Surfing the expanses of the Internet, rejecting everything which struck me as conformist, I found three associations which were sufficiently marginal: the National Bolshevik Party under the chairmanship of Eduard Limonov; the "Hurrah!" Youth League under 29-year-old Sergey Shargunov; and Heydar Jemal's Islamic Committee.

I needed weapons, people, the invasion of a sovereign state. I needed extremism. After reading about these three organizations, I concluded that the one closest to me in spirit was the National Bolshevik Party. That conviction was strengthened when I discovered that several people, including Limonov himself, had been arrested in 2001 in the Altai Mountains and charged with illegal possession of weapons and attempting a revolutionary invasion of Kazakhstan. In 2007 the party was declared an extremist organization and officially proscribed. No, I wasn't about to join. That would be to seriously undersell myself. I had no intention of becoming just another brick in their edifice. I wanted to exploit their power to my own advantage. There was a call on the NBP website for everyone to assemble at noon on 16 December in Mayakovsky Square. It would be the perfect opportunity for me to meet the party's leaders and some of its rank and file and to find out what motivated them. They would ask me to sign up when they saw the scale of my personality, that was for sure, but I would find a suitable pretext to decline. Not least because, having scoured the world map at great length, I had put an 'X' on the territory of a certain country. But all in good time!

6

If you do not know what to do and which of two alternatives to choose, at least behave honorably.

Observing life in those few days of December before the time appointed, doubts suddenly crept into my mind. Every now and again my father's words would re-surface. I was conflicted. Each of us is several different people. Gorky wrote that different personalities co-exist in us, three, even four. We are obliged to make a dispassionate choice in favour of one and to crush the rest without pity. I was perplexed now by the possibility that one of those I was asphyxiating might have been the best of them, the good, positive person I could have become.

And now a second question confronted me, as if a light bulb had lit up above my head the way they do in American cartoons. A very bright light bulb. What if my father was right and I really should live respectably, like normal people do. They live and enjoy the life they've been given and become successful in their chosen craft or profession. The modern world offers many opportunities, so perhaps I should just choose whichever one most appealed to me. That was how one aspect of me argued, one of which I had been unaware. It wasn't even a line of argument, just something wondered aloud, the words spilling out and scattering like seeds of doubt in my mind. I needed to make a choice I thought I had made long ago. If I were to plunge forward now, to choose the path of resistance, turning back would not be an option. I was standing at a crossroads.

Time flows. You will remember we mentioned that earlier. I and my doubts were carried along in its flow, and then it was 16 December. It was unforgettable. Excited, confident, obstinate, I headed off to where the action was, despite the warnings, despite the fact that I was well aware I had only to shake the hand of any one of them to get my name on lists, in archives, dusty files in secret repositories. At some point in the future that handshake would be there, waiting to pop up and cause me aggravation.

All these entirely justified misgivings receded the moment I saw Moscow was on a war footing. Hundreds of people in uniforms, one every few yards along Mokhovaya Street. Manege Square cordoned off. There wasn't space for a mosquito to emit a quick whine among all the greatcoats and huge vehicles parked everywhere and anywhere. Each of these monsters contained twenty or thirty plump OMON riot police, crash helmets and all, smoking edgily and swearing. There were barriers everywhere, bewildered tourists, and up in the sky the clatter of a helicopter. It all seemed like one of my dreams.

My resolve had almost drowned in the stomach of the underground transport network, but my mind recoiled from the idea of retreat and freed me to go to where my heart was bidding me. That was the moment I made my final choice, on which there is now no going back.

From the Nationale Hotel I made my way up Tverskaya Street. Boutiques, restaurants, newspaper kiosks, everything familiar was suffused with something unfamiliar. A shirt with intricate patterns in a shop window hadn't changed since last I saw it, yet now it seemed quite different, not how it had looked yesterday or the day before, or when it was first arranged in the display. Different. This differentness was everywhere. Everything was imbued with change. On Tverskaya itself there were army vehicles of various descriptions, mainly khaki, but some were blue with barred windows and the word 'Police' painted on them. There were what at first glance seemed to be ordinary buses, but the bodies moving about inside them were wearing military uniforms. Huge antennae mounted on specialist vehicles reached out a dozen hands in different directions. On the roof of a Gazelle truck a policeman perched, looking into the viewfinder of the video camera presciently mounted there and pointed in the direction of where I was going. By the red painted headquarters of the Mayor of Moscow, from whose balcony, a plaque reminded us, Lenin once spoke, a young soldier was trying on a backpack with an aerial only too familiar from films about the Second World War. Behind the Podium jewelry store, as if trying to hide, fifty riot police were on duty, their trousers tucked into their boots and their helmets the size of ripe watermelons.

Some loser was cleaning the windows of the jewelry shop with a special mop, a sponge neatly attached to a long thin pole. By his feet, a red bucket filled with murky water stood on the pavement of Tverskaya. "How can anyone be cleaning windows with all this going on?" I looked at the road. Hundreds of cars sped Muscovites in both directions.

"How can people be going about their business with all this going on?" I looked reproachfully at the window cleaner, a scrawny little man with a wispy moustache. "What can I do about it? I've got a family to feed," he thought apologetically, I thought.

Tverskoi Boulevard was blocked. The usual party of power had settled there, posted throughout central Moscow by their unknown warlord. I had almost arrived. I needed only to get through to Mayakovsky Square, the epicentre of events which promised to culminate in an outburst of street fighting.

Here we shall do well to turn for a moment from the military force and focus on the figure I cut. I was clad in tight black trousers, a black turtleneck, a black sailor's sheepskin jacket, black hat, and brutal pointed boots I had burnished before setting out. My black bag, which usually felt so heavy, today was weightless. I felt elated, and seemed not to be walking but hovering a couple of feet above the ground and moving my legs only in order not to attract attention. In this manner I proceeded from the Modern History Museum to Mayakovsky Square. God grant I get the chance to experience that buzz at least once more in my life.

Here the military stood shoulder to shoulder. Faces lined the full 500 metres or so of the pavement. As if on parade, they stood solemn and resolute, but registering no real understanding of what they were doing there. There were almost no pedestrians. I would even say, I was on my own. All those who were supposed to be at the protest were already there. Others had probably chosen different routes. I was alone with the army and we were not on the same side.

I knew that in all probability every one of them was a perfectly decent guy. They all had their own life story and it was only circumstances obliged them to stand there, obeying orders from superiors rather than marching with me and others to demand a revolution, to create one. I walked on, feeling like a doomed revolutionary on my way to the firing squad. The eyes of all the soldiers were on me. Entering into the part, I walked a little taller, added to my expression a hint of ruefulness at being thus caught, and a little disdain. At the same time, I was thinking, "Don't worry, guys, I don't hold this against you. You are only doing your job. Everything's cool." They all admired me, I thought, my dignity and bearing. I wasn't weeping, wasn't sniveling or trying to find a way out, but marching contemptuously towards the scaffold.

Having proceeded 200 yards in the guise of a tragic captive, I was suddenly transformed into the leader who had forced the regime to take such meticulous precautions, cluttering up Moscow with military hardware and the people who serviced it. I became the visionary politician, a living legend, whom chance circumstance had caused to be late in coming to head his rebel army but for whom self-sacrificing people were waiting in the square, people willing to die for my ideas, for my person, and for the order I planned to establish. This role suited me no less than the previous one. The roles came to me of their own accord, imposed on me by my heart. I could even feel the cold metal of a pistol tucked into my trousers and concealed by my jacket. What sort of leader doesn't carry a pistol? Of course, when the bullets started flying in my direction, valiant men would shield me with their own bodies, saving my life as they perished one after the other. Later I would weep at their graves and pray and award them posthumous honours, but not just now. Just now we were joined in a decisive battle and there was no place for tears.

When I suddenly became transformed into the rebel

leader, the young soldiers whose eyes had been following me also changed. There was more contempt in their faces too, but in most of them I read, "It is my duty to despise you now, but when battle commences we will all come over to your side and support you!"

In Mayakovsky Square the speaker was saying into his microphone, "The regime is scared of us. It is a cowardly regime! We shall return to this place! We'll be back!" Thousands of young throats picked up the refrain: "We'll be back!" Someone in the crowd shouted "Re-vo-lu-tion!" and everyone shouted back, "Re-vo-lu-tion!" The December wind fluttered banners, red and white, black and white, orange. I had arrived precisely as the protest was ending.

Journalists from TV companies I didn't know were speaking into microphones, reporting to their fellow citizens on the events taking place. The riot police started flexing their muscles in anticipation. Someone unfurled a white banner above the rally with black lettering which read, "Welcome, March of Political Prostitutes!"

"Provocateurs!" said an old man standing next to me. The protestors shouted, "Get stuffed! Get stuffed!" at the provocateurs and there was so much energy in that chanting, such enormous power!

I was looking for Limonov. I wanted to see him. I intended to meet him, or someone in the party leadership to contact him through them. I had studied their faces on the Internet until I could recognize the party's entire executive committee. There were a great many people around and to find Limonov was practically impossible, particularly since I couldn't actually see any of the leaders. As I made for the exit from the rally, I pulled myself up on the stone wall of a building in the hope of getting a better view. Two lads passed me. One, a short young man wearing a dark blue cap, boasted, "I gave an interview." "Who to?" "The Russian Service of the BBC." "Oh, the Russian Service of the Pee Pee Sea," his friend mimicked.

Strange-looking people in black, wearing headsets with microphones, were, as if just for their own home video, surreptitiously filming those leaving.

Limonov's supporters appeared under their banners, but none of those in the front row were the party's leaders. They were rank-and-file members with armbands, a few of them masked, and some without distinguishing marks of any kind, moving along Brestskaya Street.

I joined this motley crowd of members of an officially banned party. They were chanting "Power to the people! Power to the people! Power to the people!" And "Putin out! Putin out!" A helicopter hovered overhead. Suddenly, our orderly ranks wavered. Ahead I could see clashes. Those in the first ranks carrying banners started fighting back with their flagstaffs at the attacking riot police. Some, as always, tried to run back but others ran forwards into the melee.

They started to crush us. The small group I happened to be with was blocked in and not allowed to move forward or back. I was afraid of a stampede, because I would take the full brunt of it, standing right next to a wall.

"What's going on?" I asked the person standing next to me.

"I have no idea," he said with an embarrassed smile. He must have been fifty or sixty years old.

I had a feeling that all those who were being blocked in were just the hapless protestors they arrest as 'criminal elements' in order to meet some target. Try telling them you were only a bystander! I could imagine the face of my parents if they found out I had been arrested at this march, after our conversation. I tried to persuade myself I didn't care in the slightest what my parents thought. If you worried about upsetting them and always followed their advice, you would never make your own way, and end up living conventionally. I tried to set all such thoughts aside.

Suddenly there was movement and everybody was running back towards Mayakovsky Square. Behind barriers and the backs of the police, journalists were photographing and recording everything. In order to get clear of the crowd, I moved right over towards the forces of 'law and order'. Coming round a group of people, I glanced over at the journalists ... Damn! One of them was filming me with a hefty camera perched on his shoulder. I stepped in a puddle with my boots, which until now had been as black as deep, dark caves.

Walking back to Belorussky Station, I took the Metro a couple of stops and was soon home. Russian TV said not a word about what had happened. I turned to Euronews. In a handful of people kettled against a wall by the riot police I glimpsed the top of my hat.

7

I hate cheesy boys and pert, pretty girls who smell of expensive perfumes and drive around in large cars with tinted windows. With wads of money in their designer label bags to satisfy every whim, they have all you need: money, girls, shooters, nice gear. They have all the things which shouldn't belong to them. In their hands are all the things they don't deserve but which give them the right to sneer. This youth category may not yet have proliferated in Russia's towns and villages, but anyone who lives in the megalopolises will know exactly who I mean. Their unattainable lifestyle is screened by clouds of hookah smoke in prestigious cafes, restaurants and clubs with strict 'face control'. If you haven't pinned on a couple of stylish items with loud-mouth labels, that is no place for you. In their world, everything matters except your heart. Which mobile phone you have, which gem that is sparkling in your lughole, whether your ass is clad in something from the latest collection: it all comes together to create a single picture – your image, which many mistake for the human being. If any element of your composite image fails to pass face control, everyone will identify you as a fraud. It is a very attractive world, which is why such crowds of people are trying to get in. It is a world without care, and the anxieties to which all flesh is heir drown in loud music and laughter. Rows of white, even teeth flash. Breasts in décolleté, more captivating even than those on display at the Nobel Prize award ceremony we attended, every now and again pop out in the course of dancing while their owner is in no hurry to put them away again. She is young and proud of her youth and attractiveness. She dances her ritual dance, assiduously shaking her ass in its sheath of sheerest denim. The straps of her G-string panties now and again fleetingly remind the world of their presence, if they aren't already being purposefully paraded above jeans level.

The principal error of these folk is to suppose that life will pass in the form of one big party, a chaos of unending celebration. Heedless of the future, they burn the candle at both ends here and now, day and night. And yet, even the prettiest of today's girls will age and cede her place to some new young creature.

There are huge numbers of them. You need only go to *www.damochka.ru*, a popular dating website, to see a constantly replenished column on the right. They pay for a slot for the next few minutes and their photo appears on the home page to blight the mood of every visitor to the site. Guys feel obliged to be photographed with their car, preferably with the Russian flag emblazoned on the registration plate, and making a sign with two fingers at the camera. Girls press and squeeze their breasts, grimace and pout lips painted with lip gloss, as if to demonstrate to the visitor that here is someone who sails past bouncers, a member of the elite. The girls are often kissing each other but "it doesn't mean anything". They arrange invitations, mobile phones, diamonds real or fake in a small heap, photograph them and send the end product off into the big wide world of the Internet.

Of course, some of them are impostors in fake Chinese or Turkish Dolce&Gabbana, claiming to seek a one-to-one relationship and posing with second-hand mobiles, but they are doomed. Even if they get past the bouncer, their inauthenticity will be detected the minute they are inside. They need either to stay on the sidelines or kowtow to whoever they went in with. He who pays the piper calls the tune.

Why should I pretend? I am writing this only because I don't get in myself, and because I envy them their being so carefree, their opportunities, and their girls. That's what I hate. "What makes them so special?" I sometimes ask as I look at their pix on the Internet. Mansions furnished 'to international standards', Porsches, BMWs, Mercedes, girls who wouldn't give me a second look sticking out their tongues, squeezing their tits, and so on down the list. What my parents earn in a month would barely buy these people a T-shirt. I hate them for their unassailability, for their supposed superiority. I hate them for not being me. But then again, there must surely be something more behind that carefree front, something deeper than their playthings, more important to them than mere chic accessories.

Time, to which we pay so much attention, brooks no exceptions. It can't be bribed or tricked into stopping. They will grow up, have families and no longer need their parties. They will call it re-thinking their priorities. That's actually what they say: "I've grown up. I've re-thought my priorities. I'm a family man now. I'd do anything for the sake of my family." Brightly coloured sound-and-light disco music, heart-pounding bass are no longer what they live for. Emancipating themselves from one addiction they replace it with another. They start a career, and the champion cocksuckers of the holiday scene (forgive me, impressionable readers, I have to write frankly) are transformed into respectable mothers who teach their children not to pick their noses or fart out loud.

No, I, Artur Kara, am not of their number. Rising above them, I scrutinize their lives through the microscope of my talent. For the present I excel them only in the strength of my spirit, but the hour will come when, through the power conferred by my deeds, valour and integrity, I shall outshine them in material terms also.

Palaces await me with luxuriant gardens, marble fountains, oak pavilions and dear, good friends with whom I shall share my home and converse about the soul.

8

Have I told you how much I love books? Very much indeed! Their fine bindings so agreeable to the touch, their pages white and thin or slightly yellowed and bulky. Every one of them, I believe, has a soul and this book of mine too, of whose cover I as yet know nothing, nevertheless also has a modest soul. Doubtless I am writing it because I have something I want to say, and have invested some part of myself in its numbered pages. It is, after all, not everyone who would sit wakeful at three in the morning in a striped shirt with the sleeves rolled up, wearing a red-ribboned hat and white shorts in order to write about how much he loves books and their "fine bindings so agreeable to the touch".

Bookstores are my element. I know the layout of their floors as well as the subject specialists, – where you will find religion, where poetry or drama. If you are seeking August Strindberg ask me rather than the badged know-nothings the shop provides to help you. "Who? Strindberg? What kind of books does he write?"

I love to stroll among the thoughts of clever men and women, conveniently displayed on the shelves of lofty bookstands. I love to touch them, to browse through them, to buy those which suit my mood and, having bought them, immediately start reading them. To be delighted or disappointed, to become absorbed or bored. The writers I read with particular reverence are those whose books I feel I might have written myself. My thoughts are set down there, even though the author died long ago and his body has decayed in the earth of distant lands as yet inaccessible to me. Some day I shall visit the graves of these authors and, laying a hand on their headstones, will converse with them, exchange emotions, study the houses they lived in. In just that same way, perhaps, impressionable readers will some day converse with me, and I shall be watching with a smile from a world beyond the grave, as those other writers, I am sure, are watching me. Sometimes, the most heartfelt of their words reduce me to tears. Turning off the light, I water the pillow with my tears as I speak to them. Quite often they understand me better than the living and I hear their words through the starlight, in the vigil of the moon, in the silence of my room, through the emptiness. Through eternity.

You may not remember the names of their characters. To your shame you may forget even the major events of the plot, and yet retain in your heart some aching sense of involvement. You may recommend them to your friends long after reading their books. Literature lives to engender this feeling in the reader, and not for the sake of story-telling, which is neither here nor there. That needs to be understood.

Dead writers, like any other artists, are more monumental than those still living. Alive, they are much like anybody else, but in a portrait they appear sublime. Standing next to one you appreciate, of course, that you are in the presence of a living classic, but closer inspection reveals he has hair growing out of his ears. When his image is a hundred, or preferably two hundred, years removed only what most matters about him, his essence, will remain and what was going on in his ears will be long forgotten. I will yet compose my ode to Death, but I'm not planning to die any time soon, no matter how great I am.

I came out of a bookshop the other day and was walking down Bolshaya Dmitrovka Street, on my way to living my life. On the other side of the street, but walking in the opposite direction, came Sergey Shargunov wearing a suit and carrying a folder. It was as if God was egging me on, as if to say, "Okay, then, now try your ideas on him." I instantly recalled that all the major historical figures firmly believed they had been chosen by God. It is true, people like us have an invisible mark on our brow.

Hurriedly crossing the road, I called out in delight, "I know who you are!" It seemed to me he flinched. "You are Sergey Shargunov, my favourite author!" I continued, implementing my plan. We shook hands. "Why were you so jumpy when I came over, Sergey?" I asked familiarly.

"It's dangerous. There are Nashists about." As if to emphasize the point, he looked around anxiously.

"Well, I'm certainly not a Nashist," I assured him, adding just to myself "Although I am a great writer and future president of some state or other". Aloud I said, "I just love modern Russian literature. You're a great guy! Would you like me to tell you all about yourself?" Shargunov dissolved in a smile of self-satisfaction. "You won the Debut Prize and transferred the $2,000 prize money to Limonov, who was in jail at the time, right?"

"I was in correspondence with him then."

I can't deny that Shargunov has an aura, and his smile, self-satisfaction and amiable bragging all appealed to me. He could be a friend.

"I'm looking for a coffee shop on ... Street. Do you know where that is? It's just that I have to meet someone there and I've been wandering around looking for it for twenty minutes."

Having vouchsafed him my recommendations on how best to find the desired destination and wished him a pleasant evening, I received a coveted name card.

"Be sure to phone! We need people like you," he told me.

"Right, I'll be sure to! See you soon!" We shook hands again, now more firmly, as comrades.

I was pleased. A swarm of thoughts were buzzing in my head. "He has the contacts I so much need at this stage. He could easily introduce me to Limonov." Another plus for me was his relative youth. It should be easy to find a common language with him, and not difficult to win his confidence. The ability to take risks, courage, passion and a will to see radical changes, all of which would be very helpful to us, are most often found in young people.

9

I often dream I am among the greats.
To catch the likeness now the sculptor strives
Of one sublime who sits and contemplates,
And understands the meaning of our lives.

I often hope I'm not just one more slob,
But if not destined for this life, then who?
I feel my Adam's apple softly bob,
Which is evidently what it's made to do.

I often pray that on this Earth
A brother shares with me these dreams,
But I'm alone, an enemy from birth,
Who watches life, which onward streams.

The others have so little hope.
The masses' future looks so bleak.
What should I do, just sit and mope?
The masses do like being weak.

I suddenly saw that before I could start to change the world, I needed to change myself. I looked in the mirror. Hair long, over my ears. Skin, not smooth, with blackheads and blotches. How come I never noticed this before? How can you rise up against the world if you can't even conquer your own shortcomings? Nails cut short, but a lot of ragnails making my hands look uncared for. I took off my shirt and patted my stomach. Oh, dear. Someone with a belly like that is only fit to stay at home, guzzle beer and goggle at the telly, not to attempt regime change.

Is that really how a man as great as me is supposed to look? No, and again no! Suddenly, in a jiffy, I found myself overwhelmed by self-loathing. Everything was wrong. I couldn't stand the sight of myself.

I went into my room and looked around. What an environment! It was a dump! Dust swirled in the corners, the table was piled high with stuff. Illuminated by the light in the room, which contrasted with the darkness outside, I saw myself in the window: a hairy, disagreeable-looking guy with badly kept nails and a flabby belly. My faded T-shirt and over-laundered shorts had lost whatever individuality they had ever possessed.

A cry of protest welled up from the depths of my soul. Everything had to change and it had to change fast! I tore off my worn-out clothes, seized a pair of scissors and rushed to the bathroom. Lock after lock, my hair fell to the cool, tiled floor. I was in a frenzy, and must have been pulling my hair too hard or cutting it carelessly. When I could no longer grasp any more, I threw the scissors to the floor in the wake of their victim. Hair, a lot of it, was piled around me. Incredible to think I had had so much! What had it all been for?

I peered at myself in the mirror. That there had been a change was not to be gainsaid. My deep-set, angry eyes had become clearer, quite unlike the eyes hiding behind that scruffy fringe. My facial features stood out more sharply, the strong cheekbones, the pointed, resolute chin. My elongated nose was in evidence as never before. That was how I now saw myself. I ran a razor over my remaining hair, repeating this straightforward operation until none remained. I brushed off the last of what was now mere trash and suddenly felt ... so alive! My scalp seemed to have become the focus of this new life, of my vital energy. There was warm, crimson blood on my hand. When I touched the top of my head I saw I had cut myself.

Immediately my imagination pictured an army of infections eager to invade my young body, but now all that belonged in the past. That was the thinking of the old Artur Kara, the daydreaming slob. I was a different person now and must not forget it. After this chapter, I shall be the man I have always wanted to be, a pitiless, angry, cunning revolutionary. But also a subtle and talented writer. And also a vulnerable human being. Was I getting carried away? The infection? Ah, yes. My chest tightened with anger, at my fears, at my superstitious worries, at my lack of faith that God had chosen me and that I was predestined for greatness. The Creator would not allow me to die before I had accomplished what I was destined to achieve.

Grasping the bottle of vodka provided for the purpose, I lavished it on my scalp. My skin was burning. I thought it really would ignite and I would see blue flames reflected in the wall tiles, but instead my eyes filled with tears. No crying! Ti scopo la mamma.

I lay down on the bed and covered my face with my hands. I would wake up a different person.

And yet, despite the perfection and beauty of the story you have just read, I could not sleep. Like a searchlight directed at my window, heedless of the tightly closed blinds, a bright light invaded my space and dazzled me. "Can the cops really have sussed me already?" I wondered, shading my half-closed eyes in the manner of an American gunfighter.

"What cops? What are you on about, you pathetic cinéaste?" my inner voice quizzed me querulously. "What do you mean, what cops? They've detected the threat I pose to society and have decided to carry out a pre-emptive strike! All is lost! My ambitions are in ruins, and I haven't even written my book!" I retorted. "You wish, asshole!" the voice hissed, and was heard no more.

Watching myself as if filmed in slow motion by multiple cameras, I first lowered my feet to the cool floor. Continuing to shield my eyes, I threw back the blanket. My skin was immediately covered with goose pimples and contracted into a tight wetsuit several sizes too small. My nipples hardened and the hair on my arms and legs stood on end. A strange cocktail of emotions swept over me, which consisted of fear, anger at the fear, apathy and resentment. In an instant I was at the window.

The light struck me with redoubled force. I abruptly pulled the cord of the blinds and fixed them in the raised position. My eyes closed, my hands on the windowsill, I was completely exposed. The light shone through my eyelids. A sense of tranquility suddenly flowed over me. My head span and my legs gave way. I sank slowly to the floor and lay flat on my back. The kindly voice of a wise old monk instructed me, "Cross your arms as though in death. Be not afraid." I wasn't afraid. I took no interest in whose voice that was nor in where this strange shining was coming from. I just did as I was told, mechanically, not thinking normally, full of confidence that it was the right thing to do.

I sensed that I was rising from the floor and flying somewhere. A warm breeze caressed my scalp. Thousands, hundreds of thousands, millions of rose petals moistened my entire body. I fell down, sinking into a mound of petals. Their yielding softness welcomed me, their scent inebriated me. There was no escaping them...

10

I am six years old, a good boy with full cheeks and lips. Everybody loves me and I don't believe I will ever grow up. I believe that cannibals used to live in the yard next door before they were caught, and I believe in Grandfather Frost.

I also believe my parents will live forever, and that babies are brought by a stork or found in a cabbage. My name is Artur and I love the world! I love life and I love people. I love military parades and my kindergarten. It seems to me that the outside world consists only of my courtyard and my kindergarten, though in principle I do know there are other countries. I often go out to play in the yard, to climb in the playground, to play with friends at dirks, tag or football. If there is no one in the yard, especially on hot summer afternoons when I really want to play, I pull myself up on the horizontal bar. My mother says this is good for me, and what she says is right. I also have a leather jacket and heaps of leggings which I wear when I'm taken to the kindergarten. I would go there on my own because I'm big now, but my Mum says it's dangerous to cross the road, and what she says is right, you know.

If I go with my parents to the Nest of Gentlefolk bread shop through the back yard (which is shorter), I get to go on the swings. We haven't got swings in our yard because somebody broke them, but I'm not cross with whoever did that. Who cares! There are other swings anyway in one of the yards if you're going to the Nest of Gentlefolk and we do go there, to get bread.

Sometimes, when there are lots of children in the yard, we play hide and seek. First, we decide who is going to be 'It'. We decide that either by eeny-meeny-miny-mo (we have several counting rhymes) or playing stone-paper-scissors. The person who is It has to stand by the wall, fold their arms, close their eyes, count to ten and shout "Ready or not, I'm coming to get you!" In different parts of the yard you can hear children giggling. They all try to hide really well because the person who gets found first will be It next time. I usually scramble up on top of the red garage. From there I quickly climb on up into a tree which has branches spreading over the garage. I lie face down on a big branch and hold on with my little hands and let my legs dangle down both sides. It is a very good place to hide. The other children don't usually look up, so often I have to come down myself after everybody else has been found, but it means I get to see the whole of the game from start to finish.

I love animals too. We have a cat. She lives near our door and often has kittens, but they almost never live for even a day before they die and my dad goes off to bury them. My sister and I cry in our apartment, because the first time we saw her kittens one morning my parents promised that if any of them survived, we'd take one home. But the kittens are always dying and we are always growing bigger and don't cry as much as we did the first few times because we've stopped hoping.

There is a lot I could tell you about what I like, what I don't like, about my life at home, in the kindergarten, about my friends. I could give a detailed description of each of them and of the chewing gum I love so much I often ask to have it as a birthday present; and lots more, but then I would wander away from the main topic of this chapter. I would break the link which binds me, lying in rose petals raining down on me, to things which happened thirteen years ago.

That was when I first saw a dead body. It was one of those hot days when you can't bear to be sitting alone at home and you go out to join the boys and girls in your yard but there's no one there. I hung from the bar, testing my willpower until my hands slipped off of their own accord and I fell to the ground. I didn't feel like going home, there was nothing to do in the yard, so I decided to play in the stairwell and climb up to the ninth floor at the very top. Stepping out on to the balcony of the highest floor in our district, I liked looking down at the road. I wasn't so bored if I was looking at the cars driving along and the occasional passers-by.

As I climbed the stairs I was singing a song I can't remember now with a voice I no longer have, but when I got to the top I was struck dumb. A body was lying on the concrete floor. I rushed back downstairs, but when I had got my breath back a flight below I gave in to my curiosity. The stranger was in the same position as when I had left him. I crept closer, afraid all the time that he would grab me with his strong, hairy arms. He wasn't even breathing. His stomach wasn't rising and falling, and when I went closer I saw his face and his neck with a trail of blood on it. Blood had dripped down to form quite a big puddle. I ran downstairs in horror.

I found refuge in the strong embrace of my mother and told her all about it. The police took the man's body away and maybe caught his killer. What kind of state was I in? Tears of terror choked me, tears of astonishment and revelation. So that was death, right in front of me. It wasn't a movie where, after a successful take, the actor gets up from where he has died and goes to wash off the greasepaint and ketchup in the shower. There had been a man here, and suddenly because someone else willed it, he wasn't there any more. For the first time I became aware of how precious life is.

That night, swaddled from head to toe in a blanket (which made me feel safer), I suddenly saw clearly that some day my parents wouldn't be there any more, my friends wouldn't be there. I wouldn't be there. One day we would die. My tears flowed even more uncontrollably and I gave out a weird wail.

When the gentle, wrinkled hands of sleep had dried my tears and wiped my nose, I found myself in a forest. The treetops were swaying in the wind. Branches waved to me. The sky was as blue as could be, completely cloudless. I was standing in lush grass and wearing my favourite leather jacket. A squirrel scampered by and I could clearly hear the sound of an invisible ocean, the breathing of its waves.

Set among the trees was a white swing. I ran to it in delight. It seemed to have been made and set up here specially to wait for me. I swung so high I started seeing my feet against the treetops and the sky, then relaxed. The swing went on carrying me up and down. I was really enjoying being among all the scenery, breathing the air, seeing the sky. I felt the fullness of life and forgot all about death.

Only, I had a strange feeling someone was watching me. You probably sometimes have the same sensation. You are alone but you have a feeling that someone you can't see is hiding behind a particular bush, a particular tree, a fallen log. There are movements you can't explain around the suspect objects. A cone falls from the tree, something stirs the bush.

Meanwhile, the smooth motion of the swing had weakened and almost stopped when suddenly the trees which, up till then had been densely surrounding where I was, parted in front of me and created a curious path. It was straight and I couldn't see an end to it. I got up in amazement and took a few steps along it. Someone was coming towards me from the other direction, silhouetted against a dazzlingly bright light.

"Look away," a deep voice commanded, a voice which seemed to hold all the world's knowledge and power.

I did as I was told, because I couldn't make anything out anyway. I was completely dazzled by the light.

"Do you know who I am?" the voice asked.

"No." I was scared.

"Well, I'm God. You may have heard about me."

"Yes," I said, "I have."

"Well, what I want to tell you is this. Firstly, don't worry. This is only a dream, and the moment you wake up you can forget all about our conversation. It's up to you. But secondly, I have summoned you for a reason ..." I pinched my arm, trying to wake myself up. "Stop pinching yourself! You will wake up only when I decide it's time you did."

How had he seen that? For heaven's sake, I was standing looking away from him.

"Don't try to work out how I saw you pinching yourself. It makes no difference that you've got your back to me. I see everything, even when I'm not beside you. You will see a bright light sometimes. That will not always be me. Sometimes I shall send you instructions. Try to get used to that light, then you will be able to understand it."

"What's the light for?" I made myself say, in order not to seem impolite. "That is how it must be! Once in a hundred years I give them a hero. That's the deal. So then, don't be afraid of anything. Follow the dictates of your heart. And as for your mum and dad, don't worry. When they become old and weak, I'll find a good place for them. 'Bye now."

My heart was pounding. I jumped out of bed and fled like a rocket to my parents. Only sandwiched between their warm bodies did my heart rate return to normal. Although, of course, it was only a dream, I remember it to this day. I was six years old, and I was a good boy with full cheeks and lips.

11

Leaving Chistye Prudy Metro station in central Moscow and strictly following the instructions I had been given, I took a tram. Its stuffy metal belly took me to the agreed stop. After roaming about for a bit, I found my turning and, walking through some back yards, found the right house.

It was one of those early autumn days when summer is only just over and hasn't yet been finally replaced by autumn. It was a kind of demi-saison of light jackets, clean shoes and back-from-the-holidays faces. The entrance door confronted me with an unwelcoming entry code panel, but you didn't need to have been awarded the Nobel Prize in Literature to identify the three buttons which had to be pressed simultaneously to release the door magnet. They are always more worn than the others. I went up to the second floor, conscious of mild excitement. Standing in front of the right door, I inspected myself, brushed imaginary dandruff from my shoulders, and rang the bell.

The door was opened by Fatima, whom I already knew. Clad in the style of a strict Muslim, she gave me such a broad smile that she unintentionally displaced her green scarf which, when she stopped smiling, obediently returned to its place.

"How did you get in?" Putting on one slipper, she hopped a couple of paces and looked symbolically into the stairwell. "Was someone coming out?"

"Well, no, Fatima. I just pressed some buttons I liked the look of, said 'Open Sesame' and the door obligingly let me in to my Muslim brothers and sisters." Fatima giggled. I looked around. "Nice place you've got here."

Despite her entreaties, I did take my shoes off. Nobody offered me tea, because it was the holy month of Ramadan. "Heydar isn't here yet," Fatima said, gesturing to me to follow her deeper into the apartment. She turned and added, "But some of the boys are."

Opening the door to a large room for me, Fatima departed. I sat down in a massive black leather armchair and surveyed my surroundings. The walls were covered with plates painted with Arabic script, and on the few bookshelves I could see the spines of books in Arabic, Turkish, English and Russian. A table stood by the window, presided over by a computer. I could tell from the sound of the hard disk that it was switched on, but the monitor was turned away from me and I quickly lost interest in it.

The room was fairly bright, despite the absence of the traditional chandelier. There were only a few floor lamps on the dusty floor. The walls were hung with round wooden plaques with Ayat from the Q'uran painstakingly inscribed on them.

Often at such moments of stillness, foolish thoughts are fired like an arrow into the bark of consciousness, making you edgy and irritable. So now, I suddenly got it into my head that if anything were to disappear from the table, or a bookshelf, or anywhere else, after I had gone I would be considered a thief. My imagination rapidly sketched in a beautiful ring with a huge emerald lying unsupervised beside the computer when I came in which had now suddenly disappeared.

My anxieties about the existence of such a ring were interrupted by the 'boys', as Fatima had called them. "Assalamu alaikum wa rahmtullahi wa barakat!" one of them standing in the doorway intoned and held out his hand to me.

I shook it and replied, "Wa alaikum salam!"

"Assalamu alaikum!" the second man greeted me.

"Wa alaikum salam!" I repeated, and energetically shook the hand extended.

"My name is Airat," the first, a well-built man aged thirty or so, introduced himself. "And this is Rustam," he said, indicating his companion.

"Pleased to meet you, all the more so since my brother's name is Rustam. I am Artur," I duly introduced myself.

Airat sat down at the computer and Rustam sat on the floor, leaning against the wall with a proprietorial air. After an awkward silence, during which everybody smiled and looked around, Airat said,

"While we are waiting for Heydar to come, I will tell you something about us. At last the Islamic Ummah in Moscow has its own organisation, the Islamic Committee under the leadership of Heydar Jemal. He will tell you about us in more detail, so I'll just give you a general idea. You made the right decision in coming here," he began his recruitment speech. "Where is a young Muslim man to turn in a world where everything is controlled by infidels?" Seeing me frown, Airat qualified his remark. "Well, I'm not saying that all non-Muslims are bad people, – that would be foolish – but you know yourself that it would be equally foolish to deny that at present Muslims in Russia are disunited. We are not using our full potential. We are not allowed to hold key posts." He paused, rubbing the light stubble on his chin.

Then Rustam took over. "You, for instance ... we can see from your eyes that you are an intelligent person, but you need to consider what prospects you have in this country. Of course, you can find yourself an isolated niche in the system, but it seems to us that we should move beyond being little local satraps." The reader will notice that Rustam was speaking metaphorically, but his thoughts were nevertheless wholly intelligible to his listener. "A Muslim could never become president, say, or prime minister. He will not come to power because he is surrounded by non-Muslims who, for generations, have occupied the key posts." Rustam moved to a chair next to Airat, before going on to say, "Yet there are, according to various estimates, between 15 and 30 million of us in Russia alone, and we have every right to power."

Propping my sceptical head on my fist and inclining it slightly, I was unconvinced by their propaganda. In the first place, the Minister of Internal Affairs, in charge of one of the most important departments of the Russian state, is a Tartar; and secondly, it is simply wrong to talk about a world in which "everything is controlled by infidels", as Airat had carelessly put it. According to the tenets of Islam, Jews and Christians are People of the Book. I had no intention, however, of sharing my thoughts with them. I kept on the mask I had donned the day I made my irrevocable decision.

"Yes, absolutely. How pleased I am to have found my way here!"

Rustam and Airat exchanged glances, pleased with this result. There was a pause.

"Well, let's get to know each other better. Tell us who you are and what you do," they suggested, putting an end to a silence which was becoming oppressive.

"I matriculated at the Institute of Oriental Languages this summer. I'm studying Arabic language and history..."

"Mashallah!" Airat exclaimed.

"I'm interested in religion, politics and literature. By the way, I have brought a book to present to Heydar," – I tried desperately to remember the patronymic of the man I had come to meet, but failed. "What do you think, will he like it?"

I took from my bag a book about the former Chechen president, Djohar Dudayev, published in the mid-90s in independent Ichkeria. Airat leafed through it with interest:

"Yes, it's a good book. It even has documents." He handed it across to Rustam, who inspected it briefly before also concluding, "Yes, he should like that."

We relapsed into a state of burdensome anticipation.

The time came for us to break our fast and we went

through to the kitchen. Of course, I hadn't been observing it. I had eaten quite recently, and before ringing the doorbell of their apartment-office had had to spit out my chewing gum, but it would have been against my interests to admit it. I dutifully ate the date offered to me and washed it down with water. After that we had tea and biscuits.

Someone phoned Airat. When the call was over, he started discussing with Rustam what he ought to do.

"The questions that Gonopolsky asks! He turns everything you say inside out!"

I discovered they were talking about a radio interview they had been invited to give on "Echo of Moscow".

"What do they want to interview you about?" I asked.

"Well, what should we say..." Rustam began hesitantly.

"Go on, tell him," Airat prompted.

"Airat and I were held at the US Guantanamo Bay prison in Cuba." "Wow! How did you end up there?"

"Well, we just ... you know..." Rustam's eloquence and metaphorical thinking deserted him. "We fought with the Taliban in Afghanistan." "You mean, on the side of the Taliban?" I asked.

"Yes."

I found myself in the presence of heroic people. Those who fight for the weak are always heroic. People who live for an ideal, and do everything they can to make it a reality, are heroes. There can be all sorts of ideals, but they should be focused on the broad masses of the people, not on yourself, the person fighting for the ideal, or your family, not for your own self-interest. That's what distinguishes someone who's a hero from someone who isn't. It doesn't matter what the ideal is, and if it is brutal, that only makes it more interesting.

Heydar finally arrived. A big man with a neat goatee and shaven head, he looked imposing.

"Assalamu alaikum!" he greeted us and, after being introduced to me, asked, "Have you broken the fast?"

"Yes, literally ten minutes ago. By the way, 'Echo of Moscow' called. They want Rustam and me to do a live broadcast with Gonopolsky," Airat reported.

"When?" Heydar asked.

"Tomorrow at 19.00," Airat replied.

"Then here's what we'll do," Heydar directed. "The two of you," pointing at Rustam and me, "go to my office while I have a quick talk with Airat, break the fast, and come back to you."

We did so. When Heydar and Airat came into the office, I automatically stood up as a sign of respect. When we were all seated again a silence descended, which Heydar himself broke.

"So, what do you want to know about the Committee?"

I was a little confused, but pulled myself together and asked, "What is your ultimate goal? What is it the Islamic Committee wants to achieve?"

Heydar smiled wryly and his eyes flashed like a ruby of ill omen. "Victory over the infidels, global war, a battle between the civilisations of East and West under the banners of religion and the Imam Mahdi, who will return at the time of the Last Judgment to lead our ranks and prepare the Earth for Al-Qiyamah, resurrection, and establish the final pure religion. That is our ultimate goal."

I almost choked at the scope of their ambitions. "The Mahdi? But to the best of my knowledge, nobody knows when he will come."

"Nobody knows? The sign portending the Mahdi's return will be 'the general invasion of the Earth by evil, the victory of the forces of evil over the forces of good. This will necessitate the manifestation of the ultimate and final Saviour. If that fails to happen, all mankind will be engulfed by darkness."

I thought about this as Heydar, getting into his stride, continued, "In the words of Ali ibn Abi Talib: 'At the coming of the Mahdi people will neglect prayer, squander the divinity which is conferred on them, legalize untruths, practise usury, accept bribes, construct huge edifices, sell religion to win this lower world, employ idiots, consort with women, break family ties, obey passion, and consider insignificant the letting of blood.

"Magnanimity will be considered as weakness and injustice as glory, princes will be debauched and ministers will be oppressors, intellectuals will be traitors and the readers of the Q'uran vicious. False witness will be brought openly and immorality proclaimed in loud voices.

"The sacred Books will be decorated, the mosques disguised, the minarets extended. Criminals will be praised, the lines of combat narrowed, hearts will be in discord and pacts broken. Women, greedy for the riches of this lower world, will involve themselves in the business of their husbands, the vicious voices of man will be loud and will be listened to. The most ignoble of the people will become leaders, the debauched will be believed for fear of the evil they will cause, the liar will be considered as truthful and the traitor as trustworthy.

"They will resort to singers and musical instruments … and women will ride horses, they will resemble men and the men will resemble women. The people will prefer the activities of this lower world to those of the higher world and will cover up with lambskins the hearts of wolves.

"The Mahdi comes to reestablish the lost sense of

sanctity. Firstly, he will reestablish Islam to its original purity and integrity.'"

"That time has come," said Airat. "God's laws are violated massively. People have forgotten their destiny. The Truth, I mean."

I was crushed by the atmosphere in this room, the inscriptions on the walls, the semi-darkness which had gradually replaced the earlier brightness, these faces, the burning eyes of the leader of this whole enterprise, the words he uttered. I found his words oppressive, not least because they did not fit the framework I had constructed in the course of my own elaborate mental exertions.

"But how will we know the Mahdi has been born? I imagine people have repeatedly claimed to be the Twelfth Imam, just as the Cossack leader Pugachev claimed to be Peter III, Emperor of Russia. I ask so that we can protect ourselves from being taken in by a pretender."

"You are the product of a civilization which calls everything into question, but it is a valid question. Well done! They say that 'At the moment of birth a light pierced the top of the child's head and reached into the depth of the sky. This child is the Mahdi, He who will fill the earth with equality and justice just as it is now filled with oppression and injustice'."

Lean, haggard Rustam was sitting on the floor, propped against the wall and either contemplating the bright times to come or his own heroic past. Airat for his part was staring straight at Jemal's lips. I was amazed by the spiritual purity of these people, with which my own sordid motives in coming here were in terrible contrast.

"From what we know from the Q'uran and Hadith of the Prophet, sallallahu allayhi wa sallam, we can say that during the reign of the Mahdi power will be taken from non-monotheistic and materialistic unbelievers and given into the hands of Muslims and others of this world who are worthy of it," Heydar said, concluding, "And the last shall be first."

"It's time to pray," Rustam announced. Everybody got up. I was terribly embarrassed, and cursed myself for having stayed so long and for the fact that, even though born a Muslim, I still did not know how to pray.

"I don't know how to perform namaz," I confessed, without any expectation of sympathy, indeed, expecting to be driven ignominiously out of their close circle.

After a moment's thought, Heydar said, "You don't? Then imitate everything we do."

Heydar and Rustam discussed at great length who should act as imam in our collective prayers: that is, who should stand in front of the rest to lead our prostrations. To my surprise Heydar was treating sinewy Rustam with immense respect, probably because of something in the past. At all events, it seemed not to occur to him to invite Airat to lead the prayers. In the end, Heydar allowed himself to be persuaded and took his place in front of us.

Airat disappeared into the depths of the apartment and emerged in the company of Fatima, who brought us our prayer rugs. We each took one and spread it before us. I find it hard to describe everything I felt, imitating the actions of genuine Muslims in their communion with God. My actions appeared to be sinful, but on the other hand they seemed merely comical. To anyone watching, my tardy reactions must have seemed like a bad parody, but I was calm because, even if I was committing a sin, the fault lay with Heydar, who had pushed me into it.

After our prayers, Heydar took up where he had left off. Inspired by his own hopes, he said, "Our banners must fly above all others. Gradually increasing our numbers, constantly gaining new supporters, increasing our power, we shall come to represent a real political force whose opinion counts. The regime will be afraid of us, it's true, but we shall have the intellectual power of our leaders, our personal spiritual strength, and ultimately the divine power which instructed us to begin this war!"

He carried on talking, but I gradually stopped listening. Instead I looked at his stockinged feet with the toes awkwardly tucked underneath. I peered at his bald head gleaming in the semi-darkness of the room. It was the head of a dreamer, whom you should first hear out, then gently hug, show him the kindness he has probably never been shown, give him a tranquilliser, and every day bolster his faith in his own destiny.

"The country we live in is controlled by the state bureaucracy, for which the owners of private property act as economic servants! We need to be clear in our minds that, under a system of bureaucratic absolutism, the right to own property is reduced to a mere convention: an owner is an owner only as long as he is a 'cash cow' for some bureaucratic power group."

Suddenly, unintentionally interrupting Heydar, Fatima brought another 'brother' in. We all shook hands and the boy introduced himself as Togrul. With glossy black hair and wearing a black uniform, he cut an imposing figure. He was between twenty and twenty-two, about the same age as me. His body language soon made it clear that he was not yet an initiate of this movement, which was evidently extending its influence. He viewed us as 'old wolves' who were specially knowledgeable about something. The conversation which followed confirmed my impression of him.

"Okay, then, tell us who you are, what you do, what you're passionate about," one of the captives of Guantanamo repeated the usual questions. The boy answered thoughtfully and conscientiously. He had just completed his course in legal studies at one of Moscow's universities and was now looking for a cushy job. Of course, he didn't actually say that.

What he said was, "I have read your writings," he glanced respectfully in the direction of Heydar. "They seem close to my own feelings and I would like to learn more about the Islamic Committee."

Those were his words, and I interpreted them as my cynicism prompted me. For some reason they did not tell him, as they had me, about the Committee's global ambitions, but limited themselves to plans for the immediate future and the demands they would put forward.

Something I didn't like, both in respect of myself and of Togrul, was that they wanted us to involve other people.

"We're planning a series of lectures on 'The Meaning of Time'," Heydar Jemal said. Rustam and Airat seemed to be in a trance and just sat there looking distracted. "Bring your friends and acquaintances, mainly non-Russians or people who take an interest in politics."

"'The Meaning of Time'?" I repeated, much taken by the splendid title and the profundity of the topic.

"Yes, the meaning of time," Heydar replied. "I need to go to Baku ..." As he mentioned the city his eyes filled with a good kind of warmth which showed how much it meant to him. "I need to think everything through."

In his thoughts he was already there as he sat hugging himself, lost in thought. He was already sitting in a gazebo on the shores of the Caspian Sea, gazing at the horizon and the sunset, or perhaps a picturesque sunrise.

He had some intimate mystery which he had been cherishing all his life, and for me it was obvious that within that massive body of an intelligent politician was concealed a, certainly courageous, undoubtedly heroic, but nevertheless vulnerable soul, sensitive and even delicate. In that, he reminded me of myself.

As we were about to leave, Heydar called for application forms for joining the Islamic Committee.

"Well now, since you share our ideals and are willing to fight for them, sign up now." He jabbed a chubby finger at the bottom of the form.

I had anticipated his move and politely refused, stating that, "A single conversation does not give a full picture of the matter." I paused before continuing. "I need some time to think over the meaning of the future transformation." I then concluded unabashed, "I am not a superficial person, and before I act I need to understand fully."

Airat, Rustam and Heydar found my answer satisfactory, and I thought saw me as, if not an equal, then an almost equal 'player' on the stage. Togrul hastened to follow my example, and while we were putting our shoes on in the hallway, Airat even came to say, "Well done, lads! You've made a good impression!"

Heydar was more restrained, but he too clearly felt we had something valuable to contribute. "Be sure to come to the lectures. You're welcome in this house any time. From this day its doors are always open to you."

That really is what he said. Rustam said nothing as he shook hands with us, and for some reason I had a feeling that he alone understood my true intentions.

Having been given copies of a pamphlet entitled "Manifesto of the New International" and "Program of the International Social League", I went out into the dark city. I changed my mind about giving Heydar the book on Dudayev. It no longer seemed appropriate.

On the way home, I read the pamphlets carefully. I

really think the programme of the League deserves to be adduced here in full, but will limit myself to a few quotations. For example, the second paragraph of the Program reads: "The revolutionary struggle of the International Social League aims to take political power away from the lumpen-bureaucratic state and give it to the people, thereby returning basic political power to the public with guarantees against future attempts at misappropriation. As a revolutionary force, the ISL aims to make the most basic democratic representatives of society the sole source of the political initiative which determines history."

It also proposed complete eradication of the "lumpen-bureaucratic regime", to declare its executive institutions criminal, and hence to consider the regime's juridical basis without legitimacy. Consequently, all organisations "whose activity is in any way sanctioned by the regime and which serve its purposes" were to be dissolved and banned.

I wasn't too sure what was meant by the lumpen-bureaucratic regime, and hadn't a clue about some of the other terms. The anticipated "future attempts at misappropriation" were fairly baffling, but I liked the programme overall.

"The political class of the Russian Federation, which includes the core official bearers of executive power, the organisers of the appropriation of social output, managers of security institutions, and the providers to the executive branch of ideological and propaganda support services, must depart the stage of history without heirs or assigns."

The main "object of alienation in a bureaucratic society" was stated to be "the object of the Law". There then followed an entirely logical explanation, to the effect that the Law as a juridical object was the corporate property of the state bureaucracy in its policy of imposing total political domination on a particular country. Moreover, the right to determine political legitimacy also passed into the hands of the bureaucracy.

As a result, it was proposed that in the Russian Federation priority over all other forms of expropriation should be given to expropriation of the Law, "which becomes a platform for restoring other aspects of violated justice in both the social and material spheres". Expropriation of the Law from the bureaucracy which has privatized it "betokens returning historical initiative to the public sphere".

I found the program as interesting as I found it unrealistic. Reading this product of an undoubtedly talented person, I had the clear impression that the world depicted in the ISL's Program was destined forever to remain a figment of its creator's imagination.

I was also fully aware that the provision that "any community is free to govern itself to the extent that it does not undermine or violate the Universal Social Charter", a charter intended to replace the Constitution, was entirely unfeasible.

I needed to rip and tear down and bomb today, now. I could not afford to wait for decades. I intended to see my whole enterprise through to completion in a few years' time. I wanted a platform for speeches, hundreds of thousands listening, hundreds of thousands of valiant soldiers praying for the victory of old men ... and I needed it now, without recourse to the chimerical dreams of a reincarnated Mahdi who would help me along, without relying on expropriation of the Law occurring of its own accord as a result of my speech.

Casting the pamphlet aside, I started thinking about the undercurrents of this movement. The International Social League and its slogans were universal in their aspirations and could appeal to more people than the ideas proclaimed to me in that gloomy apartment at Chistye Prudy. I found an unacceptable ambiguity in their ambitions, but if that ambiguity would have speeded the attaining of the admirable goals this revolutionary group was aiming for, it would not have bothered me. I would have quelled my doubts and invested all my energy and abilities to achieve those objectives. Their cause, however, was close neither to me nor to the people with whom I intended to surround myself. I would almost go so far as to say that Heydar Jemal was their only genuine advocate, the only person who really believed in the success of the enterprise.

Before going to sleep, I wrote in my diary, "Heads, shadows, talk, eyes, bursts of indignation, moments of outrage, seconds of misunderstanding, things left unsaid, and blatant propaganda: all of them were present in our revolutionary circle."

12

Boys and girls, teenagers, standing in photographs behind gnarled leathery fathers and mothers, give me hope. Their eyes look mistily and rapturously to the future. One should live for their sake.

Eduard Limonov

To flow like oil over the smooth white marble surface, to frame yourself with congealing brown blood, to seem still alive, still metabolising. Especially if you feel the heavy lead in your head, the ringing in your ears, the sharp knife puncturing an outlet for your natural feelings.

To examine yourself in your last moment and think perhaps about something heroic – Revolution, say. To fall back finally, emitting a wild cry, to bid the world farewell.

To decompose in the damp earth, not even knowing the gravestone from which people will read your name.

I had a long argument today, for some reason in English, with a fellow student who claimed the life of the masses is not meaningless. He resorted to highly sophisticated rhetorical techniques and gestured energetically. I could see how worked up he was, how much the topic mattered to him. About parents he asked, "Do you think that your parents live without purpose?" et cetera. He tried to argue that the meaning of life is reproduction of the species, and that because generations increase and family trees ramify, people's lives do have an end result and ultimately make sense.

I countered, albeit regretfully, that the bulk of humanity live their lives to a large extent quite senselessly, just eating, drinking, shitting, and possibly loving in the process. That is, they perform a succession of natural human functions. I forgot to mention working and watching TV. I said this was a value system unworthy to exist, that everything must change, including people's consciousness. You cannot fritter away life, which we should be marveling at, on such trivia. It is unforgivable! To disappear without ever having known yourself, to leave behind nothing of value! To be a useless burden occupying one square metre of ground. To be mere flesh and bones travelling the world.

I was very disturbed by this conversation and for a long time afterwards paced the corridors deep in thought. To hear a young person talk like that! Students have always been an active political force when it comes to principled protest. Alas, they too have been tamed. They too have been domesticated.

This evening I went into the woods to think over my plans. I needed to understand the cause of my early failures. It was time to draw up a preliminary balance sheet. I have talked to enough people, honed my rhetorical skills on them, but from time to time I have let myself down, failing fully to gain their trust. They have retained a shadow of doubt, even though I can see right through them. Even at the University, this guy, who didn't just look stupid but really was as thick as planks, was like a great boulder which I hadn't the strength to budge. I couldn't shift him from the fixed position on which he had constructed his whole outlook and life.

Dressed in funereal black, I went through to the family room.

"Where are you going? There are so many drunks in the streets! Some day you're going to find yourself in trouble!" My mother issued her stock set of warnings, which never stopped me from going out.

"I'm going out for some fresh air!" I said, reaching for my socks. I glanced at my watch. Half-past eleven.

"You always go out so late! You're just asking for trouble! Couldn't you have gone for a walk earlier?" she asked, tearing herself away from the television screen for a moment before once more succumbing to its allure.

I put on a pair of new black shoes and went out. I was met by a cool breeze from the street. Crowds of drunk people were wandering about in search of entertainment. See the use they make of their lives. A crowd of ignorant morons getting pissed in the world's biggest country!

Among those in party mood were some teenagers who didn't seem overburdened with intelligence. I mingled with them, wondering what kind of thoughts they had, if any. I wondered what they would make of my own thoughts. Three kids started following me, sniggering smuttily and talking louder than they should have about other boys. Who are you, all you Petyas, Seryozhas and Vityas? What are you and where are you sub specie aeternitatis, against the vastness of the Universe?

As for me, habitually ignored Artur, I looked down at myself from the height of my destiny, at my lonely, melancholy progress through this crowd of ignoramuses, and tears came to my eyes. When I had had enough of their sniggers, I crossed the street. I saw a crutch lying on the grass and, on an inexplicable impulse, picked it up. I moved on, forcing my way past all these dickheads with their 'normal' preoccupations, leaning on my crutch.

I came to a deep lake and suddenly felt bereft. There wasn't a soul in the dark woods. The moon's reflection was dancing on the water. Somewhere, in one of the villas almost certainly owned by a millionaire, loud music was playing as I stood on a bridge above the lake. I stood there, leaning on the railing, looked over in that direction and wept.

"Take me in! Take me in to your happy, ridiculous life where you have so many friends, so much alcohol, where marijuana is a guest as frequent as in a police station, where there are no problems, and any there are are effortlessly banished! Take me in to your world of money, babes, and company cars!"

I hoped one of the revelers might come out to the lake for a smoke, notice my forlorn, crippled figure outlined against the dark woods, the water, the pallid moon and invite me over. I so love company, you know, even though I never get invited to anything. Nobody came out, the party carried on, and would have continued in just the same way if I had stood there till morning, indeed till the end of time.

"Oh, God!" I cried out as I went back into the darkness of the woods. I fell to my knees. "Dear God, I know you are near me! I know you are here, closer to me than ever in this dark forest! That is why a foolish, animal fear of some unknown monster has crept into my heart! There is nothing there, I know. It is you who are here. Send down your grace upon me and I will serve your ideals, dear God, but make me happy! Everything is in your hands, this world, their Hummers, the music, the water, the ducks swimming on it, those girls whom you created, all religions, the Mahdi your messenger. Nothing is impossible for you!"

A gentle autumn wind swayed the trees and I listened to their whispering. It didn't make any fucking sense at all. I chucked the crutch into the nearest bushes.

"In this world man is on his own! He is infinitely lonely in this idiotic, heartless world where one is always surrounded by people and rarely has a chance to retreat from everything, and yet in reality one is alone. We are born alone and we die alone, only co-habiting with someone, sharing our life with them, and finding in that the purpose of our existence."

Okay, I need to work on formulating my ideas more precisely. That will come. I'm working on it. That is my mission and I will yet be heard. If I'm not heard, I'm ready even for that.

When I got home I went to my LiveJournal and started typing, fast:

"An empty avenue of trees in autumn. Hardly surprising. It's late, especially for walking out. People like to stroll in the evening, after school or work, swigging beer from glass bottles, putting an arm round their girlfriend in an easy, uninsistent way. Good for them, all those who walk out in the open, by a pond or river or in the woods. There are fewer of them than there are habitués of cafes and restaurants, or of that simple, free and most popular pastime of all, television. Some (many) don't need anything more.

Their wages (winning the lottery as an option), the food they can buy with their wages; the friends they drink and sing songs with and in front of whom they fall asleep in the posture of someone who's made it; the wife – a haven for the wayfarer who has strayed in life; children to perpetuate the race, your blood, the purpose of life for many; the toilet to make space for the next intake of food; the shower for, well, everyone knows what for; clothes for maintaining one's social status in the circles one moves in. Isn't that it? Isn't that all the sense life has?

Rarely, very rarely love comes your way. More often love deliquesces into vexation and hatred. Rarely, but less rarely than love, there is the discovery of reading, mostly pulp fiction, light reading which doesn't tax or upset or anger them. Everything should be in its place and conveniently to hand. How big your shack is often doesn't really matter, although everybody thinks it's as well to have plenty of space.

I often ponder this, less often share these thoughts with someone else, and when I do, even though I choose the people carefully, nobody understands. For a while we talk calmly, but then begin to argue. Our premises are different, so there's no foundation for understanding. Our backgrounds differ, our levels of self-knowledge, or cynicism. Who comes off worst? Usually me. My companion doesn't forget me. He avoids me."

I sat in front of the indifferent monitor re-reading what I had written, then decided to add, "When you sit in a yellowed maple grove and the air is growing chilly you want to cry your heart out. I always feel like crying in the autumn. Why? Because of a sadness whose source I don't know. What do I have to complain about? I am well, my parents are alive, I have enough food and drink, and yet something is missing. Sense is missing. I am insufficiently connected with the rest of the world.

I become even sadder thinking about my ineluctable ideal. I cannot repudiate or betray it, cannot cast aside my bloody destiny. Who knows how much longer I have to walk this sinful earth. I sense that I shall die young. I know, I feel it, and that I shall cause my own death. I shall ask my destiny for death.

I shall overturn grey routine and go off into eternity.

Under a hail of yellow maple leaves another lonely boy will come, with tear-stained eyes and a faith, as pure as dew, in a justice which doesn't exist.

At that moment there was no person on Earth more sincere than I.

13

Since I firmly decided where my destiny lies, I have begun to live several days in each day. I have a feeling deep inside which divides the day into four or five segments. I lose myself in each.

My first segment is routine and is usually the University. Niggling classes which suppress the personality, taught using tired old methods. In this segment I need to smile a lot to stop my brains ossifying, and to filter carefully the information offered. I have to be on my guard in this segment, which is the most dangerous. Inappropriate behaviour can produce unforeseen consequences. Several varieties of this can be readily observed in the dark corridors and stuffy lecture rooms.

The second segment is more agreeable, and much briefer. It often bisects the first, gets squeezed in. Lunch. Here too you need to laugh as you discuss the events of the first segment.

The third segment is loneliness, and it is a movable item on the day's agenda. It often supervenes around midnight. When one's ration of solitude comes late in the day it is more easily tolerated, being naturally interrupted by sleep. If it occurs during the day it is more of a problem. I adapt accordingly.

The fourth segment is meeting people, tends only to happen on Saturdays and is invariably preceded by the third. That is, meeting people is unimaginable without a prior bout of loneliness. You feel good when you meet people. You immediately experience a whole ocean of feelings which are usually dormant, lurking, just waiting for something to release them. That ocean drenches everything and the first, second and third segments no longer seem so important. Dammit, what matters is that you're feeling good right now, and these thoughts create a seductive illusion.

The fifth segment is home. Your lair. A "kingdom of distorting mirrors". A storage facility for existential boredom. All-round frustration. My least favourite segment of the day.

The sixth, sleep. Dreams in different dimensions and regions, with different people you have met, possibly as a child or only a few months ago or, sometimes, whom you have yet to meet.

That's how I anaesthetize myself.

Yes, I sometimes cry. Yes, I am lonely despite my greatness. You are probably feeling nostalgic for the great and fearsome Artur Kara you were reading about at the beginning. I'm back. I hadn't gone anywhere but just temporarily allowed myself not to give my person the attention it deserves. When I finish this book, everyone will know about me, my passions and ideals. Some will be repelled, but I shall undoubtedly gain some supporters. One time when I was travelling in the stomach of the Metro, I wrote in my notebook, "If even a third of you cast my book aside in disgust without having reached the middle, I'll have done my job well." That's absolutely right.

Hello-o, is anybody there?

Having thoroughly reviewed the situation in respect of the Islamic Committee, I decided to proceed with caution. Without repudiating anyone, without neglecting friendships with anyone, I would extend my acquaintances in these circles the better to understand each association's internal organization, in order to acquire allies, and to facilitate the invasion of the state I had selected.

My visions did not abandon me. Once when I was lying on my bed with a book, the room was lit up by a flash which dazzled me, but was less bright than on the previous occasion. Letters were again scurrying along within the flash. Oddly enough, that assemblage is still in my mind, as if someone had stamped it in my brain, imprinted the characters with red-hot metal. It was my first revelation about Sense and Meaning.

To start with, red and purple letters traced the title. It was the phrase 'Revolutionary Instant'. After that, an endless stream of narrative unfolded against a veritably cinematic background. The experience was exciting and unforgettable and a strange magic was in the air. These projections, which I took to be tricks played by my mind, mesmerized me. I couldn't stop watching them, and in any case I was enjoying the moment.

The letters, which I read to myself, sounded in my head like the voice of God already familiar from my dream fourteen years earlier. It was all completely out of the ordinary and, try as I may, I cannot find words to adequately represent what was happening. The voice announced, "One city after another was occupied by the volunteer troops of the Sensites. Some towns greeted them with jubilation while others resisted, defending the dictator's brutal regime." I watched the rapidly scrolling letters, heard them in my head, and in the background saw innumerable groups of armed men entering the various cities. Crowds of oppressed, exhausted people cheered and bowed. Some attempted to resist, but without much conviction. The power of their spirit, the power of their certainty of the rightness of the struggle, which could easily be read on the faces of the invaders, was totally absent from the expressions of the defenders, and I instinctively sided with the attackers. Of course I did: I was watching my dreams come true.

"It seemed that the invincible pyramid of power con-structed by that man could withstand the blow of any force but the Sensites did not believe that. Their only doubt related to the steadfastness of the people. Would they give active support or merely robotically applaud the daring of the rebels, of which nobody could any longer be in doubt? The Sensites did everything in their power to win full-hearted popular support. They waged their war in accordance with the best writings of the theorists of guerrilla warfare in particular, and of revolutionary struggle in general, making full use, needless to say, of their imagination."

We see the headquarters of the Sensites, as the voice calls them. People are looking at documents, discussing them, outlining something on blackboards.

"The leaders of the Sensite army were a handful of brave, dauntless, methodical people. They seemed to have come from another world. They came from the wellsprings of History. They could be killed, but their spirits then hovered above the battlefield. They have no reason to be the least ashamed. They will appear before Me with pride and fortitude in their eyes, and I shall give them their reward."

OMG! Among the obvious celebrities in this crowd I could see myself. I was older, my face tanned but less firm, my body still strong, my teeth white, looking good in my dark uniform, and ... my eyes aglow with an unearthly purity, inspired, filled with resolution. Those were the eyes of the great Artur Kara, who I am not yet but am resolved to become.

"Small units of Sensites infiltrated the state by a variety of routes, all illegal. They had no intention of supplementing the database of the country's intelligence services with their own profiles. Some in cargo containers, concealed behind crates of oranges, were brought in by an unsuspecting long-haul truck driver from Iran. Others in cheap boats landed on the coast. Arms were smuggled in by the same routes."

I am shown a map of Turkmenistan, the country I happened to choose. From Iran, from Azerbaijan across the Caspian Sea, from Uzbekistan and Kazakhstan red arrows swoop in. I struggle to make out the date of the invasion, but the font size of the inscription above the arrows is too small. History does not stand still, however, and already these frames have been replaced by others no less interesting.

"The first to rise up were the prisoners. In this country of lawlessness and state violence nobody knew for certain who had been imprisoned for a real crime."

First there is footage of Boris Shikhmuradov, the former Minister of Foreign Affairs, on a big screen, filmed during his show trial. His lips are moving, and I know what he is saying: "We are drug addicts not deserving of life" and "President Saparmurat Turkmenbashi is a gift from heaven to the people of Turkmenistan". Then there are frames shot in a prison cell, its ceiling so low that, condemned at first to twenty-five years in prison and then to life, he has to sit bent double. It is more like a dog kennel than a prison cell. And what is that on his back? I clearly see, embroidered on a patch attached to his shirt, 'Traitor to the Motherland'.

It was more than I could take and I wanted to look away, but some mysterious force held me in my original position, my limbs no longer belonging to me and my body no longer obedient.

"Having silenced the existing radio and TV stations in the country (other than satellite), the leader of the Sensites addressed the nation."

Of course, it was me, handsome, magnificent (but without narcissism). I was wearing a khaki cap and those eyes blazed out from beneath it.

"Assuming the leadership of the state for the duration of the war, he announced in which towns and cities firearms and explosive devices would be distributed. He also appealed to the army: 'You alone can prevent bloodshed. You cannot always live in fear. The former President of the Republic has been captured and will shortly be brought to trial in accordance with the norms of international law. Despite the massacres (the commission of which has been confirmed by reliable sources) carried out on his orders, despite his laundering of state funds, he will be given an opportunity to defend himself. We do not want deaths. We are all members of one family. We must live in peace, in happiness, in our own country, on the lands we have inherited from our ancestors ...'."

The leader of the Sensites will have a lot to say. The nation will sit spellbound around radio and TV sets before exploding in jubilation. There will be no better country in the world, and there will be a place under the warm rays of its sun for everyone.

After watching the final frames, I crashed out.

14

Change is what our hearts demand
Change is what our eyes demand.
In our laughter and our tears and in our pulsing veins
Change is what we're waiting for, change.

Viktor Tsoy

I arrived at Avtozavodskaya Metro station a bit too early. In response to my letter, a member of the National Bolshevik Party who had given his name as Akhmad, suggested meeting there at 16.00 hrs in the middle of the foyer. A gathering of some kind was planned and, after attending it, I was to plunge into the world of the NBP (National Bolshevik Party). I didn't feel like waiting at the Metro, not least because I needed a shit. By the escalator I noted with satisfaction seven or so policemen. Going up and exiting through the wooden doors, I encountered a further vanload of police. "That's what I call organization!" I remember saying to myself.

For a while I wandered through streets full of people and cars, looking for a suitable location to disburden myself and finding a snug toilet in a cafeteria whose name now eludes me. Emerging, looking first right and then left, I walked back towards the Metro. Two pretty girls in the window of a cafes waved and I instinctively smiled back. I spotted a kiosk selling hot dogs and screeched to a halt to buy a hot dog with ketchup and French mustard, and a Pepsi, upon which I repaired with my repast to a nearby park. I'm not really that big on hot dogs and rarely buy one, but some days that is exactly what you feel like eating. I haven't yet discovered any pattern in when these rare days occur, but that was one of them.

Finding a solitary bench and running my hand over the wooden slats to check it was clean, I sat down. The bench relaxed comfortably behind my back and took me in its embrace. I wondered what I was doing, and whether I shouldn't just turn 180 degrees, and get the hell out of there. No, it was out of the question. Not on. While fully cognisant of the advantages of 'normal' life, recognizing its guarantees of security and stability, of a measure of prosperity if one agreed to play by 'their' rules, I did not deviate from the path my heart dictated, the path to which my dreams had led me.

I took a bite of hot dog. What I really like about a French hot dog is the lack of mess. It is in a bun and has a hole bored through it lengthwise, such as a ferret might burrow through soil. This hole then has sauces poured into it to taste, and the sausage inserted. The sauce and the sausage remain sealed in the bun and you don't get them all over your hands.

Having chewed the hotdog to a pulp, I washed it down with Pepsi-Cola and tried to relax. Here, next to the park, was the District Prefecture building. Above the metal fence rose a statue of Lenin, a legacy from the Soviet era. He had one hand in the gap between his suit buttons and the other raised aloft, helping him to convince the world proletariat of its mission. Cool goatee and flat cap.

"Everything you conceived and created has collapsed, but here you still are, and in thousands of other places too, giving people something restful to look at. Your name is still emblazoned on your eponymous Mausoleum. When I went there with a group of Chinese, I bowed to you. I wanted to take a closer look but stern guards didn't allow me to move away from the walls we were being shepherded past. That's what history means!" I thought, extending my arms wing-like on the bench, with a hot dog in one hand and the bottle of Pepsi in the other. "The only worthwhile thing to do is strive to become a part of it and stay there."

Abandoning myself to less weighty thoughts, I suddenly felt sad. I mentally surveyed my situation. I had no halfways close friend, let alone girlfriend. What chance do you have of finding a girlfriend when your leg is covered in scars and you've got a limp? I had no reason to believe that love is blind. I could, of course, find a girl like myself, with some deformity, and would probably feel more at ease in her company, but the trouble was, I only fancied supremely glamorous beauties, girls whose appearance was flawless, the kind you see in music videos on MTV. To my discomfiture, there are lots of them in Moscow but none who would give me a second glance.

I did not want to be the freak I was. Yes, I was a freak, and my foot was part of it. Whose fault was that? Who had made it that way? It was evidence that God had a nasty sense of humour. Perhaps he would compensate me for playing a joke with my destiny. I often wish I could fall into a deep, blissful sleep, dream beautiful dreams, and wake up the next day physically perfect. I would inspect my foot, transformed as if by magic, step on to the cool, smooth floor, and then walk over to the mirror and, in disbelief, check myself out. Walk, you know, not hobble!

When I first arrived in Moscow and hadn't been admitted to a prestigious high school, I had to attend an ordinary local school. After being introduced to the briefly silent class, I limped over to the desk my teacher had indicated. Everybody was staring at met, resplendent in my white shirt and black trousers. They were whispering, discussing me. The girl I was to share a desk with was a large blonde called, I later discovered, Sveta.

When the commotion surrounding my person died down a bit and the lesson began, I peered blearily at the blackboard with its algebra, for which I had little enthusiasm, and felt obliged to start writing. After all the equations and rules relating to the new topic had been explained and the students had one by one, obedient to the teacher's will, extracted themselves from their desks and gone up to the blackboard to reinforce what they had learned, I tore a piece of paper off the last page of my slim, green exercise book and wrote on it "I love you". Placing the slip of paper face down on the desk, I slid it across to my neighbour.

I do not know what I hoped to achieve by my declaration of love. It seems unlikely I had any great understanding of what the words meant. More probably, this was just my way of expressing liking for someone I had seen for the first time twenty minutes before.

Sveta turned the paper over and read my confession. "Ha, ha, ha!" A burst of laughter was her response. "Ha-ha-ha-ha!" I was confused. Periodically giggling to herself, she carefully slipped the paper into her bag. By next day the whole class knew about it and everyone was laughing at me.

"You were made for each other," I was told. "The cripple and Hooky." "What do you mean, 'Hooky'?" I enquired, ignoring 'cripple', which needed no explanation.

"Hooky? Well, Sveta, of course!"

I smiled, supposing this nickname had been awarded to my chosen one for some past accomplishment. All became clear, however, when the girls were playing football.

I, Sergey the Orphan, Andrey and Roma were sitting on a bench by the school playing field, but not the way I am sitting now, eating a hot dog and ruminating about Lenin.

We had climbed up on to the back of the bench and were sitting there with our feet on the dirty seat. Four or five girls were kicking a ball about and Sveta was in goal, trying to deflect the occasional shot. "Look at Hooky," one of the boys remarked. "Why 'Hooky'?" I asked.

"Well, look at her hand," came the reply.

"What do you mean? You've got a hand as well. Actually, you've got two," I joked. They all laughed.

Sergey explained the mystery. "Look, her hand is as bent as a hockey stick." He fired back another question. "Are you saying you didn't know?"

"No, I didn't." Everyone except me had a smoke, while I stood up to peer at Sveta's hands. I immediately noticed that her sleeves seemed longer than normal. Her right hand particularly was hidden by the sleeve. A high shot at goal made her leap with arms outstretched, baring her hockey stick arm. The hand was bent unnaturally sideways, and the skin as red as if she had been scalded.

I limped home. "Yes, we're quite a couple," I told myself. "Really made for each other, the cripple and Hooky." My heart ached at the thought of my imperfection, my ugliness, from which I had nowhere to hide. I raged at myself for my weakness. Of course, being a freak was a weakness for me with my longing for the flawless, bewitching face of beauty. I have always dreamed of having a beautiful life, a stylishly furnished home, a car with beautifully stitched seams on its leather seats, a smooth, handsome face, and an irreproachable body armoured with muscles of steel. That day as I wandered home, I realized I was facing a crucial choice: 'Yes' or 'No'!

In my situation, a weakling would have clutched at Sveta, like Sindbad the Sailor clinging to a plank from a sunken ship, floating till he reaches an island. I wanted none of that island, that tranquil haven of disability, surrounded by embarrassed looks and too much attention, in the form of excessive kindness, paid to your imperfections.

For a time I hesitated as to what to text to her best friend. First I typed "Tell Sveta nothing has changed and I still like her just as much". On reflection, I deleted that and wrote: "Tell Sveta I've got a girlfriend". I re-read it, sent it, and immediately switched the phone off, collapsing on to my bed in floods of tears.

It is a hard path, in some sense the path of a Samurai, of an infinitely lonely man who has chosen to be lonely. And here that man is now, sitting in a park in Avtozavodskaya, finishing what remains of his hot dog.

My repast over, I saw it was time to join my comrades. I headed into the Metro. A few people who looked like misfits were waiting down there for the rest to arrive. Some were standing alone, others in pairs or small groups. There wasn't much of a buzz around my own, as yet little known, person, and I kept close to one of the station pillars, continuing to observe the National Bolsheviks.

One with shiny black hair was dressed completely in black, evidently following the dress code recommended in the Short Course of the National Bolshevik Party, which states, "It is preferable to dress all in black: black shoes (trainers), black jeans, black shirt (T-shirt), black jacket (best is a bomber jacket – the slippery fabric and absence of a collar will prevent enemies or the fuzz from getting a hold on you). Dirt, blood and gun oil are less visible on a black background." Others were dressed however they chose. There were several girls in the group.

What I immediately noticed was that the National Bolshevik is easily distinguishable, even in appearance, from the man in the street who glides unhurriedly through life. The disciples of Limonov, in my opinion a great writer, had an air of instability and even poverty. Poverty is no crime, but having read my fill of books about revolutionaries and any number of the manifestos they produced, I had an image in my mind of what a New Man should look like, – the representative of a species hitherto unknown, a Superman, if you will.

"I expect these are just the foot soldiers," I reassured myself. "The more respectable and better groomed supporters probably only sponsor projects, meeting occasionally with the leaders or simply transferring funds to the accounts of a party which is forbidden by law even to call itself a party."

"The National Bolshevik Party promises you, boys and girls, a life full of heroism, adventure and sacrifice, a proud and strong life and heroic death. At present, scattered through the villages and towns of Russia, isolated, you are nothing, living small, private lives. The NBP will bring meaning to your life and status in the society we shall create. You will be the elite of an Alternative Russia!" Extracts from the party program (which I had memorized) flashed through my head, a program put together over more than a decade by generations of loners.

"The Party is a powerful armament. It is both a collective and a personal weapon. It is a weapon for realizing Revolution in Russia, for creating a New Russian Nation, for building a strong Russian state. It is a gun for your personal struggle against the world. Remember that without the Party you are nothing, the plaything of others. Without the Party you have no prospect of rising. With the Party you can become anything: a Gauleiter, a general, a leader. Remember that! The Party is you!"

Fair enough, let's see what kind of party this is. No harm in taking a look.

Akhmad finally arrived, wearing cheap, light blue jeans pulled up to his belly button and with his shirt tucked in tightly. Starting with me, he greeted everybody there before coming back to me.

"Nazir will get here soon. He's from Dagestan. You're from there too, aren't you?" *Ciao Bella io ti conosco*

"No, I was born in Grozny." *Tu fiuli canella mandala*

"You're Chechen?"

"No, a Kumyk." We stood for a time.

"Well, it looks as though we're all here. Let's move. Anybody who is late knows the way and they can come in a separate group," Akhmad announced, moving round the circle of Limonovites.

"No, that's not safe. Let's wait a little longer," said a tall, bald guy, who for some reason everybody called 'Mohawk'.

"Okay, Mohawk. We'll give them another ten minutes," Akhmad agreed, and checked his thinking against the testimony of his watch.

"Hey, your name is Akhmad but you don't look like an Akhmad," I shared my own thinking. "You don't look like you come from the East. In fact, I would even say you look decidedly Slavic."

"I converted to Islam quite recently. Before that I was called Pavel."

I remembered that, of course, Limonov in his sensational article, "The Islam Card", had written that Muslims should make common cause with the NBP and urged them to join up. He mentioned Heydar Jemal in it, whom I now knew, and said it was Heydar gave him the idea. He concluded the article with the words "And may Allah be with us".

"Why Islam?" I was interested to know how

consciously this straightforward Russian boy had made this choice. It's not everyone converts from the religion they were born into.

"I read a lot about these things. And then, if you look at it from a purely logical viewpoint, Islam is the most complete religion, and Muhammad (may the peace and the blessing of Allah be upon him) is the Seal of the Prophets. Islam does not deny Judaism and Christianity. It recognizes the Torah and the Bible as holy scriptures and Moses and Jesus as prophets, but Islam is the final word."

I said nothing. It is a bit awkward when someone who initially belonged to another religion is more knowledgeable about yours than you are yourself, and more sincere in his dedication and more devoted to his faith.

As if reading my thoughts, Akhmad-Pavel enquired, "Do you go to the mosque?"

"Well, you know, sometimes," I fudged. "I went to the shop at the mosque with my father several times to buy meat." Involuntarily lowering my eyes, I asked him in turn, "How about you?"

"Of course. We meet there every Friday."

Another group of National Bolsheviks finally turned up, Nazir among them. In his black trousers and blue shirt, with a black beard merging with his moustache and deep, rather beady black eyes, he looked every inch the revolutionary. He glanced at me with curiosity looking into my eyes for a few moments before Akhmad-Pavel introduced us. "This is Artur. Remember, I told you about him. This is Nazir Magomedov. He's a student in the History Department at Moscow University and concurrently leader of the National Bolshevik Front there. All the National Bolsheviks studying at Moscow University are under Nazir's authority."

We shook hands. I immediately took to him. Calm, confident, mindful in every step he took and every word he spoke, he instilled trust and wiped out my initial misgivings about the thin, dusty NBP members. I would be able to get on with someone like him. I could entrust someone like that with one of the fronts of Sense, because I could already see in his eyes the look of a Sensite, of a person capable of dedicating himself to an idea advanced by me, and prepared to see it through to the end with me and other heroes like us. I call us heroes without irony, as you will see.

After a certain amount of small talk, I started asking him about the aspects of his life that I was interested in: what had motivated him to join the Party and how he saw his future in it.

"I arrived In Moscow three years ago," he said. "I came to study history at Moscow University, and have been a party member for two years. First, I read some books by Limonov, then I got interested and checked out the Internet, and now here I am."

"Listen, Nazir," I said, adopting a confidential whisper as we were coming out on to the street from the depths of the Metro. "A lot of people accuse Limonov of nationalism, even fascism, hostility towards immigrants, and so on. I've seen a video from the 1990s on your site, where he is declaiming from a stage something along the lines of, 'Russians are entitled to their own country! Let's clear out all the occupying forces who have taken over our markets, our shops, every aspect of life ...' He rounded it all off with a fist raised in the air and that notorious slogan of 'Russia for the Russians!' What do you think about that? You are, so to speak, a recent arrival yourself."

Nazir gave a half-smile as he tried to explain. "That is a very old video. Ten years have passed since then and the situation has changed. Limonov himself has changed in that time."

"What has changed?" I ventured to interrupt the leader of the Moscow University front. "I can understand a teenager changing his ideas, being tossed from one notion to another, not knowing what to choose, but we're talking about a grown man here. His ideas really ought to have formed long ago and he ought to be defending them against all comers. Today he writes about the 'Islamic card' and calls on us to support him, but tomorrow, after he's come to power here or just in some outlying republic, what's to stop him from abandoning us and showing exactly what he meant by 'Russia for the Russians'?"

"He wouldn't do that. The grassroots National Bolsheviks wouldn't let him!" Nazir said bluntly.

I wasn't surprised, I was flabbergasted. A party which is accused of being virtually a sect worshipping its Leader and all the rest of it, a party which I had supposed had a top-down 'pyramid of power' culture, had people like Nazir in its ranks. People whose views differed in many respects from those of their Leader. You heard how confidently he said, "The grassroots National Bolsheviks wouldn't let him!"? He stated it as fact.

Meanwhile, we had arrived at our destination, which on closer inspection turned out to be the Municipal Committee building of the Russian Communist Party, which kindly made its premises available for the weekly meetings of the Moscow branch of the NBP. We went upstairs to a bright, spacious hall with a lot of seats. On the wall behind the podium, facing out into the hall, hung a portrait of Lenin, caught in an inspired pose by an unknown artist. He looked in no mood to compromise.

Sitting at the back beside Nazir so that I could see

not only the speaker but also the audience, I continued to observe. Boys of the familiar type, girls who looked like boys, a girl with a shaven head and a pram in which a baby National Bolshevik was fidgeting. The hall gradually filled up.

Akhmad finally came out to the podium. Half hidden behind it, he looked important. I liked his speech. He spoke about progress in signing people up to join the NBP, about pressing issues like membership fees which, as became clear from what he said, few people were paying, and about party cells in the regions. He was well informed about everything, was Akhmad-Pavel. He had all the figures, the names, the percentages in his head, filed away on the shelves so that he could pull just the dossier he needed out of the relevant stack in his brain. He constantly reinforced his speech with facts, which gave it substance.

"He speaks well," I said to Nazir, and he nodded approvingly.

When Akhmad finished his contribution, a girl with a solid physique was invited to speak. She was wearing the regulation white top and black bottom. A round red badge with a black hammer and sickle was pinned to her shirt collar. I immediately had the feeling I was in an archive newsreel. Although the National Bolsheviks rightly try to distance themselves from any sort of comparison with the National Socialists, in spirit at least, I detected, on the one hand from the newsreels and on the other from this meeting, that there were unquestionable similarities. They were subject to the same surveillance, arrests, bugging, there was the same air of conspiracy. You could believe that masked men might be just about to burst in, tie us all up and exile us to Siberia for 'dissidence'. All this, of course, gave me considerable satisfaction. For a while I felt a chill in the pit of my stomach. The blonde girl's mouth was opening and shutting, presumably emitting sounds I didn't hear, people were shouting something from their seats, and everyone was laughing.

I was completely self-absorbed, cut off behind the heavy curtain of my dreams of the day when I too would be the instigator of events of this kind, and these kids, or kids like them, would do my bidding, go through with them for my sake, and sacrifice themselves to my cause.

I heard on television today that in China a person only becomes a true personality after passing through several stages of self-improvement. First, on becoming a student you must have a respectful relationship with your teacher. (This relationship is rated far more highly in the Middle Kingdom than even the relationship with your parents.) Then you must become a teacher yourself, and only then will you be truly a personality.

I think that is generally the right approach. Parents cannot always be successful instructors because, driven by their emotions as parents, they try to realize in their child everything they themselves were unable to achieve, or to embody in him everything they could never hope to become. It is not unusual for a reasonably independent-minded child to choose a profession his parents find wholly unacceptable and to achieve tremendous success in it, having in the process had to sacrifice relations with his family. It is a truism that expulsion from the tribe is the lot of heroes, followed by a later triumphant return.

School teachers and then university lecturers have long been failing to fulfil their true purpose. Placed from the outset in an absurd situation, they gain influence solely by exercising their right to award grades. Take that away and see what their pupils will do to them! That is not applicable to all of them, of course, but to the vast majority, who are not teachers of life but only teachers of a subject.

A day before this meeting, I had read to my mum excerpts from Limonov's *Alternative Russia*:

"It is very common for children to be depressed by the ordinariness of their parents. They would like their father to be a hero – a champion boxer, a revolutionary, a KGB general, a freedom fighter, even a gangster. Instead they are faced with a slob sitting on his bum eating dumplings. Most children resign themselves to the mediocrity of their parents, but the best don't."

"No, that isn't right. He has no business talking like that about families!" my mother exclaimed in high dudgeon.

"A political party like the NBP takes a boy away from his family and gives him role models to follow and, in effect, competes with the family for the boy's soul."

Looking around the hall, I thought, "You really can't just glibly dismiss the phenomenon of the National Bolshevik Party as a fascist party, or a sect, or pin some other label on it. These boys and girls around me are bursting with energy, an angry, destructive energy, of course, not creative. Most likely they all come from dysfunctional homes. I'm quite certain the majority do. They are no worse, and probably better, than the cloned nerds in colleges and universities. They are alive. Alive! And what is giving this energy to them, and to me and to others like me is the National Bolshevik Party. Supposing, when he created it fourteen years ago, Eduard Limonov had chosen a less provocative name, suppose he had decided to call it the Liberal Democratic Party, say, or United Russia, or even Justice for Russia, that energy would still be there."

For normal society it is, of course, a menacing energy, but it is indispensable. Limonov, or The Leader as they usually call him in his party, has lived a really remarkable life which has included something of everything. Okay, so he might have had anonymous sex with men. What of it? Don't keep harping on about just that one detail in his biography. Focusing only on that, and turning up your nose in distaste just shows your narrow-mindedness. Ordinary, 'respectable' men have no fewer skeletons in their cupboards than the perennially youthful Limonov, only few of them would dare to talk about them in public.

I'm no angel myself. I stuck a finger up my bum in sixth grade out of curiosity. Yes, I took some vegetable oil, went to the bathroom and tried it. I wanted to know what was in there, at the end. Well, now I know. Am I supposed to hang myself because of that? I am a better man than many who never have and never will stuck a finger into themselves. Limonov is a haven for people who are different. Limonov gives hope. You are treated like shit at the military conscription office. Medical charlatans in the hospital won't give you the time of day. Dumb-ass college professors, learned only in how to wear spectacles, consider themselves superior to you and see you in their power. You are confronted by injustice every day, whether in the Metro, the street, or anywhere else. Many just quickly forget it, but some don't. Admirable people with a keen sense of justice, with a special aesthetic sensitivity, but most of them losers – that is the NBP's constituency. They think hard, and they fight courageously. Their numbers are few. So what if they are outnumbered by smug dullards. How many of them are there anyway? 10,000? 20,000? What does that matter? You will find them everywhere, and one of the epigraphs in my book is going to be something the Italian film director, Pier Paolo Pasolini, said: "Majorities have never been really right, only minorities."

Look at where the NBP has representatives. They are

all over the world. I know National Bolsheviks in Israel, in America and Canada, in Europe, in Dagestan and Chechnya. This is a global ideal of global freedom and total justice and it will live on after Limonov's death. One of his supporters said to camera, "The NBP is Limonov's best book".

"The family often loses to us but, to our deep regret, we do not always win. In essence, the family is a dead end. The influence of parents who are losers (and the vast majority of them are), sometimes violent sadists but more often watery-eyed masochists, over the twenty or twenty-five years a kid spends in the family environment, irrevocably destroys his virility. Most criminal acts of embezzlement, bribe-taking and theft are committed for the benefit of a family. A Russian official does not usually steal money from the state in order to blow it at posh Moscow restaurants but to build a large summer dacha, to buy apartments for family members, children and grandchildren. The new breed of Russian businessmen have banal tastes and predilections. A Mercedes for oneself, a Mercedes for one's daughter, a dacha for oneself, a dacha for one's son and his family. Of course, all this load of bollocks should have a stop put to it by revolution. But for a successful, deep, irreversible revolution, in order to bring about permanent change in society, we need to destroy its most durable molecule: the family."

My mother was in hysterics. "Get out, will you? This is monstrous!"

"There, you see, Mum? This is a book which really stirs people, to love or hatred doesn't matter! It rouses emotions, makes people argue, makes them reflect! Think how many books there are which you read and the next day can't remember what they were on about!"

"Just go away, Artur! You've chosen quite the wrong sort of person to admire! He is using you and people like you, trusting boys and girls who used to be good. If he's so sure you need to destroy the family and all that, why has he got a family himself? Why has he got a wife and child?"

"That's not the point, Mum!" I tried to communicate a simple truth. "Think more imaginatively! Nobody is planning to destroy the family!"

My mother stopped her culinary operations. "So what is he planning? He's put it down in black and white," she said in bewilderment.

"This is all just dreams, Mum. Ordinary dreams. Limonov and I and his supporters know this is all impossible dreaming, but Limonov is trying to make these dreams become a reality: the romance, revolution, the smell of gunpowder, the red flags. He makes it possible for us to dream about these things and believe that they will come to pass some day. His literary talent helps him convince people. Yukio Mishima created the Tatenokai private army in order to die magnificently in a senseless rebellion he knew was doomed to failure, to die as a Man."

I gave up at that. My mother will never understand these heroic vain endeavours. She belongs to a different age.

Before I return to the meeting of the NBP's Moscow branch and that blonde girl's speech from which I absented myself in such a cavalier fashion, let me say a few more words about Limonov, before leaving the topic for a time. All those who say he lies to his followers need only open the very first book he wrote, in 1976. In *It's Me – Eddie* you will find, for instance, this:

"'Fuck your world, which has no place for me,' I thought in despair. 'If I can't destroy it, I shall at least die romantically in the attempt, together with others like me.' Quite how that would be, I had no idea, but from past experience I knew that the opportunity always presents itself to someone seeking their destiny. I would not be denied my opportunity." This idea recurs constantly in his work, which is his life.

The girl was talking on and on. People were listening attentively to her, but having debated with myself everything that had come into my head, I was bored. I looked at Lenin, who was also laying down the law from his portrait. What was I doing here? I could be getting an education, finding a well-paid job, buying a plasma flat screen TV, a car, snappy clothes. I could be living happily in a little world I had created for myself.

Lenin was also standing in front of the District Prefecture, the powers that be, also trying to talk people round to something, and he was here too, in the Communist Party's building. When you come to think about it, is there really any underlying difference between people on opposite sides of the fence? I had no answer to that question.

The girl ended her speech and returned to her seat, accompanied by applause. Thin, dry Vladimir Abel took her place at the lectern.

"Limonov's right-hand man," Nazir whispered, before adding, "Used to edit a porn magazine".

I listened closely to the porn ex-editor. Personally, I had lost hope of getting my stories published in *Playboy, FHM, Maxim* or anywhere similar. No doubt that was why I was subconsciously expecting to hear something like, "You there, young fellow!" A finger pointing at me. "Stop sending us your stories. We are not going to publish them. You want me to tell you why? What is there to tell? You can stick your works, if they can even be called that, up you know where. They are devoid of literary merit!"

Instead, however, I heard a hoarse voice saying, "Well, ladies and gentlemen, it's good to see you at our latest meeting. Unfortunately, the best of us are not present. As you know, at the present time thirty-seven of us are political prisoners." Adopting a doleful expression, he surveyed us all. "But never mind. This persecution, this outrageous but predictable response from the regime proves that we are a strong, dangerous organisation prepared to take the lead in Russia's revolution. For the Kremlin we are Enemy Number One!" he exclaimed.

"To the death!" someone down at the front shouted. "To the death!" a couple of dozen throats took up the cry. The baby, which had migrated from its pram to its mother's arms, wailed frantically. "Quiet, quiet, shh, shh," she crooned, rocking it and looking around in embarrassment. "Well, if we've even scared little Vanya, what chance does the Kremlin stand?" Abel responded, trying to laugh it off before continuing his speech.

When he ran out of things to say, everybody started getting up, but Tishin arrived just in time and urged everyone to sit down again. "Sit down, sit down. We haven't arranged who's going to distribute the *Limonka* in which regions."

Tishin was a sturdily built man with a beard and a bald head. He looked like someone to be reckoned with. Someone like that might be a writer, a revolutionary, a boxer, anything you like other than an ordinary Joe who commutes to the same job and secretly collects plastic toy pistols day by day, like the sad hero of the film "Dust".

The party newspaper was distributed with the aid of train conductors. Tishin had timetables, a list of regional branches with the names of those who would meet the train, and a note of the number of newspapers each cell required. He would call out, for example, "Belorussky Station, 11.25 am, tomorrow". Somebody would put up their hand and Tishin would make a note of the volunteer's name next to the train number. He quite rapidly completed the lists and everyone again started getting out of their seats.

"Well, shall we go?" I asked, turning to Nazir with something half-way between a question and an invitation.

"You go on out with the kids. We have one or two things we need to discuss," he said briskly. All the heads of districts and regions or whatever they called their sub-districts crowded round Abel and started intently discussing something. The others joined the river flowing smoothly out of the hall.

Descending the dark stairs, we emerged into the brightly lit street. Beyond high metal barriers the cars streamed by. The boys and girls in the little groups which had formed back in the womb of the Metro spilled out on to the grass between the committee building and the road barriers. I had no particular wish to develop my relations with the ordinary party members, or even to take a first step towards getting to know them, and stood some distance apart, looking towards the road and dreaming of my future victories.

Suddenly, completely unexpectedly, I heard screams and an explosion behind me. I instinctively crouched down, turned around and couldn't believe my eyes. A mob of squat people wearing black masks, some armed with baseball bats, some with flares, and some even with guns were attacking the NatBols.

"Holy shit!" was all I could think to say.

They were firing at the kids! Caught on the hop, the National Bolsheviks began to retreat, running in all directions. Some daredevils tried to fight back, but what could these thin, nondescript boys do against armed Neanderthals? Everything happened so quickly that I just stood and watched, not trying either to escape or to stand up for people I didn't know. Then one of the attackers saw me and took a couple of pot shots. I jumped in the air, evidently hoping to leap over the bullets, and then he came at me. Commending myself to the swiftness of my feet, I was over the barrier and found myself racing down the road.

Finally, the attack was over and the masked clowns were disappearing round the corner of the building as quickly as they had appeared. The thug running after me stopped, confused for a moment, wondering what to do next, clear off with his pals, or catch up with me and then run away. He chose the first option, but didn't run fast enough.

I caught up with him. This time I was in pursuit. "Stop him!" I shouted to those in front as the wretch speeded up. "Stop the bastard!" I yelled. Several people, covered in blood, some clutching their heads, some their stomachs, were sprawled about on the ground. In an attempt to stop him myself, I tried to trip him but only succeeded in falling further behind and he bolted safely round the corner.

I went over to the wounded. NatBols came pouring out of the Municipal Committee building armed with sticks, some with mops, but they were manifestly too late. They ran round the corner of the building but, of course, by now there was nobody there. The ambulance turned up twenty minutes later. There were skull and brain injuries, injuries from non-lethal weapons, one had a broken arm. They were put on stretchers. One of the guys I recognized as Mohawk.

Then I noticed Nazir talking to Akhmad and glancing darkly in my direction. They talked some more and then both looked my way. It didn't take me long to work out. Of course, it was highly suspicious that this was my first time at a meeting, I hadn't suffered in the slightest, and was just a bit too aloof from everything.

"Oh, no, no, no," I said, opening my arms wide as I went over to the guys. "What are you talking about here?"

"Oh, just private stuff. What on earth happened?" Nazir said, trying to change the subject.

"As if you don't know. Some guys attacked us. Wearing masks. I was standing over there," I said, pointing to the spot where I had been watching the traffic through my daydreams. "That's why I didn't get hurt." Nazir and Ahmad again exchanged glances.

"Nazir, can I have a couple of words?" I asked and took him aside, away from mistrustful Akhmad-Pavel. "Listen, I know perfectly well what you were thinking. It's entirely understandable. Everybody here knows everybody else, at least by sight, and then someone you don't know turns up and wham! Like a bolt from the blue."

"No, no!" Nazir tried to stop me. "It's not what you thought! That's not what we were talking about!"

"Pack it in! Then you get attacked! Is that a coincidence or what? Plus no one laid a finger on me. That's a bit dodgy, I agree. And then, I was quizzing you about Limonov and his nationalism. I agree it all fits, only that's not the truth, Nazir. Don't think this was my doing."

"Of course I don't think that, brother, come off it!" Nazir, seeing my sincerity, relented, wanting to think it was genuine.

"It wasn't me, I swear. If I had called them in, would I be standing here beside you now? Would I be speaking about all this so openly? I have nothing to hide. I'm being completely honest with myself and with you." "Fine," he said and took me to meet Vladimir Abel.

"Vladimir, this is Artur. Today is the first time he has joined us," he said, introducing me.

"Pleased to meet you. Vladimir." I shook hands with Limonov's right-hand man. "Where is Limonov? Doesn't he come to these meetings?" Abel gave a half-smile. "I expect he had a very important prior engagement. We have to have full confidence in the Party's leaders." He walked off to talk to Tishin and those around him.

Soon we were back with Abel. He told us that the main TV stations were supposed to be coming: NTV, at least, and possibly the national Channe One, and Russia Channel, although that was less likely. I somehow found myself automatically among the leaders, the Gauleiters, call them what you will: Abel, Tishin, Nazir, Akhmad.

When the police arrived, they collected the rubber bullets, the flares, and made notes of everything they saw. Next they wanted eyewitness testimony and Nazir was instantly at my side.

"Artur, you're one person who saw everything. Will you give a statement?"

I recognized this as a covert test. If I were to say now, "No, brother, I don't need this" or something of the sort, that would be it. He would be 99% certain I was involved in the attack. "Well, I can, but I don't much want to. I need to get the Metro home some time soon. What do you think? If need be I will, of course."

"That would be good."

***

At the police station, in a place like a large classroom, twenty witnesses, boys and girls, assembled. The hour waiting for it to be my turn was very trying. I seemed to be in the lair of the enemy. I didn't know any of the rank-and-file party members cooped up with me, and they clearly thought they scented treason. I could see it in their eyes and hear it in their whispering, and in the fact that when they shared a bottle of Coca-Cola among themselves I was the only one they didn't offer it to. It started getting to me.

Having at last given my statement, I emerged from their burdensome company and was met at the exit by Nazir with the latest news. "They stopped their bus and they're all here now, at this police station! The word is that they're just going to release them but we've decided to put a cordon round the building. More of our people are on the way. We aren't going to watch the police let them off scot-free."

"Did you find out who they are?" I asked. "Yes. It's the government's Nashists! They were wearing T-shirts with the logo of the regime's youth movement. These scum have fighting brigades which recruit football fans in trouble with the law. They're all sorts of thugs and hooligans, justifying their freedom."

"Well they've really landed in it now! Caught red-handed!"

"That's the whole problem. They have supporters in very high places indeed, and what we're hearing is that there's already been a phone call from above ordering that they should all be released. Will you join the cordon?"

"No, Nazir. I need to catch the train. I'm late as it is."

"Okay, let me see you on your way."

We went back to Abel. "Goodbye, Vladimir! I'm sorry we've met on such a disagreeable day."

"Well, there we are ..." Abel smiled, plainly suspecting me of being behind it all. "See you again soon!"

"Say hello to Limonov from me! By the way, do you think he'll be here next Saturday?"

"I don't know yet for sure. Most probably he will. Come yourself!" Saying goodbye to the rest, Nazir and I headed to Avtozavodskaya station.

"Look, Nazir, no offence, but your people ran away, most of them. Only a very few really fought back, the rest scattered like mosquitoes. Quite a lot barricaded themselves inside when they heard the explosions."

"Well, that's how it is in any battle: some run away and some, on the contrary, rush forward to attack."

"I didn't fight. Do you know why? I asked myself whether or not I should fight for people I don't know, and I decided not to. Especially when their friends ran away. How can you justify such behaviour? The Party is not ready for revolution." I wanted to level with Nazir. "If they weren't able to fight that lot off, then what chance would they have in a clash with the army, the riot police, the special forces?"

"You see, our supporters were not expecting this form of the political struggle," Nazir explained. "They came to the Party to set up websites, design leaflets, to take part in direct action, publish newspapers, but not to fight physically, not to get hit over the head with a baseball bat or have rubber bullets fired at them. Now everyone can see that physical opposition is going to be needed. We need to create defence units, combat detachments, carry out training programs for Party members. We will deal with this problem."

"I need this man," I thought. "I need brooding optimists like him, prepared to find a way out of any situation."

"Yes, it would be good to do that before everybody is crushed."

"They won't crush us!" he declared. "They won't crush me. We are all different. It was Aristotle said that 'The city is a unity of dissimilar individuals'. It's the same in our Party."

Talking like this, we came to the turnstiles. "Okay, I'll go on myself from here," I said.

"No, let me see you to the train. What if there are some of them on the loose down there?"

"That's okay, Nazir. Everything's fine. I'll go on alone from here."

We hugged and parted, he going on towards his own destiny, and I to face mine, obedient to its dictates.

15

I had a fairly clear understanding by now of both the Islamic Committee and the National Bolshevik Party. There were elements I could take from both of them, some ideological and others with practical applications. I knew less about the third 'force', real or imagined, to which, as you know, I had assigned a special role in the Sense project. Sergey Shargunov, the leader of "Hurrah!", could help me with contacts I was going to need. He was a man who shook hands from time to time with the third most powerful man in the country, if not the second. I mean, Sergey Mironov, Speaker of the Federation Council, who limped home last in the presidential election. That's politics for you. The one who twists and turns and changes his colour like a chameleon gets state backing for his ambitions at minimal cost. But getting acquainted doesn't have to mean getting compromised, right?

After reading Shargunov's short novel *Hurrah!* I sent him a text message: "Dear favourite writer, How are you doing? How is Lena Myasnikova?! I have a few questions I would like to ask about your story. Artur." He replied with a friendly, "Good for you, Artur!"

You remember his self-satisfied smirk when I caught up with him in a side street and started telling him all about himself? You remember his eyes closing blissfully as if dazzled by the radiance of his glory?

Being a great admirer of myself, I know how to deal with guys like him. Flattery is the best way to puncture their defensive membranes. Hard, blatant, grotesquely exaggerated flattery works every time. Actually, it doesn't even need to be grotesquely exaggerated. Say a couple of kind words to me about my scribblings and I will weep tears of gratitude.

My invitation to the Moscow branch of Hurrah! arrived the very next day, the address suitably impressive: 32, Bolshaya Dmitrovka, smack in the city centre. When I arrived at the entrance, I announced my name to the intercom and went up to the third floor. Proceeding along the corridor, I soon saw bright red and yellow plaques on the office doors with Hurrah!'s slogan, "Morning! Motherland! Attack!"

I opened the door I needed and a few guys at computers focused their eyes on me. I in turn looked at all of them, said hello, introduced myself and asked for Shargunov. A boy who appeared to be smoothly morphing into a man not far off thirty, with the first intimations of a paunch and a mop of ginger hair covering his ears, smiled at one of the others and said, "That's him". The latter scrutinized me more closely than the former.

"I've heard about you! You're the fellow who stopped Shargunov in the street and told him what a brilliant writer he is!" Spreading his arms wide, the almost-man advanced on me with a friendly smile. "And I am Leonid Razvozzhaev, Member of the Policy Committee of the Hurrah! Youth Movement. Do you know our slogan?" Leonid Razvozzhaev asked for no apparent reason and, without waiting for an answer, all but spraying me with spit, declaimed in a loud bass voice, 'We shall fight despite the flack! Morning! Motherland! Attack!' Pretty cool, isn't it!"

I nodded assent.

"So, this is our office. These are our computers and phones. You're welcome to come, make domestic calls, use the Internet. It's all paid for, know what I mean?" he added with a wink.

"Couldn't be clearer," I assured him.

"Once a week we have a general meeting. We've got one today so you'll be able to see. We review the past week and plan our demonstrations."

I looked around. They were quite well set up. White paint was splashed artistically on the walls, the windows were ceiling height, simple tables, office chairs and equipment, but something was missing.

"We are the most promising youth organization in Russia," Leonid was meanwhile continuing. "The Hurrah! movement is the military and intellectual wing of the Justice for Russia party. We have succeeded in bringing together a broad spectrum of constituencies, including "For the Motherland!"; "Generation" (a nationwide public movement); "A Worthwhile Life for All"; the Student Initiatives Association; the National Heritage Support Fund for Artists, Art and Sport; and the Association of Young Scientists and Politicians."

There's something lacking, I was thinking, but couldn't put my finger on what exactly. I listened for my inner voice, trying to work out what I was finding so unsatisfactory about the 'most promising youth organisation in Russia'. I looked into the eyes of Lennie, as I had secretly dubbed him. I looked into the eyes of the others and saw the look of people who are satisfied with life, smug cats taking it easy on their own territory. There was no anger in their eyes, no desire for change or revolution, no will in their eyes, body language or words.

"Our ideology is a fusion of civil liberties, social

security and a strong state. We remember the disastrous 1990s under Yeltsin and don't want any repetition of that cynical experiment on Russia. But we are concerned about the growth of an unthinking dictatorship whose spokesmen are policemen and bureaucrats. Russia needs new people. Russia is just waiting for modernization, a historic leap forward in its science, industry, culture, and demographic. Russia is hungry for ideals of goodness and heroism," Lennie enlightened me.

"Lay off the guy with your ideology," one of the others said with a grin. "Stop trying to brainwash him and let him get behind a computer!" Carried away by the pedagogic role assigned to him, Lennie gave a nervous toss of his head, trying to shake off the interruption as one might shoo away an irksome fly. He continued, "Our activities are bold street demonstrations, ideological work, intellectual forums, recitals, support for talented ..."

"Leonid's on his hobby horse!" The guy jumped impatiently up from his chair and turned to me. "Don't listen to him, he's such a prat!"

"It's cool," I said in support of Lennie, but without declining this offer of deliverance.

"Erm, my name's Sanya," my rescuer said, scratching his closely cropped head. "Here, you can sit at my computer for now, take it easy. There's water over there, cold, hot. Make yourself tea or coffee. The teapot's over there. Just make yourself at home. Sergey will be here soon."

"Thank you." I sat down at the computer, which was open at Sanya's mute ICQ and someone's LiveJournal page with a title "A Highly Spiritual Existentialist Sleazeball". I started reading an open post.

Sanya meanwhile was patting his pockets and, evidently finding what he was looking for, turned at the door to say, "Erm, I'm going for a smoke. Take a look. It's open at the page of a certain celebrity writer."

"Is he any good?" I asked.

"He's okay, a bit up his own arse although he tries at the same time to pretend he's just like the rest of us," Sanya said. He rubbed his head and closed the door from the other side.

I got on with reading the page. The celebrity who was, in Sanya's judgment, a bit up his own arse wrote literally as follows:

Date: 2007-06-28 00:27

Subject:

Access: Public

"Dropped in today to collect Katy Gordon from her job on the box. She had some character called Nikita Belykh on her show, supposedly the director of some crap political party. Or deputy director, who the fuck cares. I read about him on LiveJournal. They said this Nikita is a snobbish cunt who wears expensive ties and super-exclusive suits. When this personage came shambling out of Katy's booth where the live broadcast was coming from, I couldn't believe my fucking eyes and only my inborn oriental reticence kept me from hooting. Picture it! You're expecting this real toff, Van Laack golf cufflinks, gleaming knee-high patent leather boots and fuck knows what else when out comes this sweaty pig-faced slob without a hint of intelligence in his fat flabby eyes gleaming dully under his narrow, sagging brow. He looked like he might start grunting any moment. He was wearing a shirt from a jumble sale, sloppy trousers and fucked out, dirty brown sandals, above which, because his trousers were too short, you could see fucking lavender (!) socks. I was sitting quite far away, but I could swear by Allah his socks were stinking because I felt my eyes stinging. I wouldn't be surprised if our Nikita isn't into visiting the sauna, beer, chicks with big tits, and cheats on his wife with a hang-dog look on his face like Ilf and Petrov's thieving Alchen. I bit my tongue and couldn't decide what to do. I didn't want O2TV's huge offices all turning to look at a guy chortling like an idiot. It was wild. Something else that's wild is tomorrow I'm going to Tula to open a brewery (I think) with the governor. Well, something like that. Whatever.

"As one of the Litprom website luminaries aptly put it, 'Bagirov is criss-crossing the whole country'. When I was asked I almost pissed myself and tried to get out of it, but I can't refuse the people who invited me for a variety of personal reasons which matter to me. So tomorrow afternoon I shall be in Tula. As if that wasn't enough, having creamed themselves gawping at my ugly mug in half the streets of Moscow, some headhunters from AST Publishers phoned. Actually, I had a first phone call from them a week ago. I conversed very politely and answered all their proposals in a lapidary manner: 'Guys, I publish with Popular Literature, I have a contract with them, so there's nothing for us to talk about.' The 'guys' evidently didn't think that was conclusive and phoned again yesterday. On the make like, the clowns. 'Eduard, there are at least two good reasons you should meet and speak to us. Firstly, we are talking much larger print runs and, secondly, advances which are of a different order of magnitude.' They offered me a cool $120,000 up front. I could only delicately grunt up my sleeve and ask them to stop wasting my time. I would never have written about this in LJ, but their doltish, tactless pushiness really got on my tits. So here's my answer, once and for all: Buddies, you know fuck-all about the current literary market even if you are fucking AST. What 'print runs' do you think you are offering? Have you even opened your fucking eyes and taken a look at the numbers in the first (!) print run of *Gastarbeiter*? Tell me honestly, have you ever brought out a book in that number of copies in your entire fucking lives? And about the bread, words fucking fail me. Firstly, I'm not going to sell out my pals for bread; and secondly, you forget who my agent is. For 120 grand I wouldn't undo my fly in front of your fucking cake-holes. You belong to yesterday, buddies. Live with it. Boom Shankar."

This guy is a real shit, I thought. What if, as he says, his face is on posters all over Moscow and the print run of his first book was decidedly large, that's no excuse to stand on his head trying to get everyone to like him and pose as something he just isn't, trying to make himself look good at other people's expense. He sounds like some Mr Big asserting his authority over crooks lower down the pecking order.

Actually, though, what about me, I wondered. Is it not the same river of shit sweeps me in its raging torrent down the road of life? Is it not the urge to assert myself, to prove something to other people, to seem better than I actually am? Even if I don't use that kind of slang and my language is more elegant and I'm trying to write a book for the ages, and intending thereby to immortalize myself in this world which I affect to despise, am I all that much better than this sad turd who seems to think he's God's gift to the world?

No, inside myself I am, of course, better. I later read his book and can say the same: my book is better than his, as time will testify; but actually, in human terms, if we crack open the walnut and compare ourselves, who will prove the more rotten and disgusting inside? I don't know. Let's face it, I've examined myself but still don't know definitively, still haven't got to the bottom of that one yet. And how will

I know? I just have to go through with that act under the banner of my movement, Sense, which, to judge by the revelations cascading down on me in the form of burning, blinding letters, is my destiny, my ultimate, bloody, destination.

I reassured myself that way. I rocked myself to sleep with thoughts of that sort, like a caring mother. Whatever I might think about this guy, right now I was losing to him. The score was 1-nil in his favour, and in favour of many others like him. I was losing 1-nil to the world. No matter how I might try, the score would always be 1 goal in their favour. We were starting 1-nil. That was my verdict. Later it would be 2-1, then 3-2, then 4-2 and so on ad infinitum, until, with one definitive act, I overturned the entire system of 'their' coordinates and emerged the winner. With tears of joy in my eyes, my blood-spattered body dead and yet myself alive for eternity, I would stride through the pages of history.

My eyes watered a little from a strange feeling which had settled like a heavy weight in my breast, and I quickly wiped them. I angrily closed the window of the 'great writer' on the screen and looked round to see whether anybody had noticed my moment of weakness. Leonid was smiling as he printed something out, and the other guy was hidden behind his allotted monitor.

The door swung open with a creak, revealing within the rectangle of its frame the slim figure of Shargunov. I stood up to greet him.

"Right, now, I see everybody is here," he said, shaking hands with us in turn and with that smug smile of his. "Welcome!"

Now I had an opportunity to observe him more closely. He was very lively. Even when he was silent, particularly when he was silent, you could sense the energy in him, that twinkle in the eyes which I so much needed in the ranks of Sense, of which more below. He had the slightly slanting squint of a warrior of the steppe, a mouth wanting to come to life, all the time eager to say something into its upper lip. With his long, slender fingers he could have been a pianist or a sculptor.

"Give me a minute, gentlemen." He took a winding route but had his destination clearly in sight as he moved in on a free computer, rubbed his elongated hands together and said, "There's something I have to arrange and then we'll go into the meeting room."

In addition to clearly fancying himself and being decidedly narcissistic, he was at the same time rather shy and modest. There is no contradiction in that, as you will readily deduce from what you know of me. Seemingly in love with myself, my genius, and my impending act of heroism, I am nevertheless extremely shy. Similarly, he too kept peeping at me, avoiding direct eye contact like a child getting used to me before picking up steam and showing off all the things he can do.

After ten minutes or so, we all convened in an office slightly larger than the previous one and with a long oval table seating twenty to twenty-five people. There weren't that many to start with but, to my surprise, the table soon had so many hands resting on it that there were no places left and some members had to stand. The sudden influx was because boys and girls, most aged between sixteen and twenty-two, arrived punctually for the meeting itself.

Seated at the head of the table, Shargunov placed a couple of sheets of notes in front of him and looked round with his trademark squint at those assembled. I was sitting on his right and looked round at them too.

"Good afternoon! I'm glad to see so many people here.

We periodically gather together to discuss organisational, ideological, personal and all sorts of other issues. For as long as we carry on doing that then, whether we meet here or in basements, in people's homes or in public squares, this movement will be alive.

"Today I would like to consult you about how recognizable our organization is to the population at large. What do you think? How well do people know Hurrah! and what needs to be done to raise our movement's profile?" He clasped his hands in front of him, occasionally stroking one with the other, and waited for a response.

Lennie decided to share his views. "I don't think Hurrah! is well enough known yet."

"Why do you think that is?" Shargunov asked.

Scratching his head, Lennie elaborated. "Well, in the first place, we haven't been operational all that long, and it is a well known fact that the first thing you need in order to establish any brand is time. In the second place, our ranks are still quite thin. And in the third place, reluctant as we may be to admit it, our movement has not done anything really high profile to make the public recognize us. All these problems are interconnected. I see the solution as being simply to carry on working as we are at present. With time, the numbers of dedicated supporters will increase and we will be in a position to organize memorable, even provocative, demonstrations."

"Splendid!" Shargunov declared, grasping his chin. "Splendid! Demonstrations. But there is one snag. While we are sitting around waiting for new supporters to materialize, our competitors will be running political rings round us. It doesn't matter how many of us there are. Just one person acting alone can do something which has a worldwide impact."

Shargunov looked at me, as he already had a few times already, but now there was something special, as if he already knew what I had in mind and was agreeable to it. He carried on. "In the interests of furthering our education, I want to read you something Abbie Hoffman wrote. Abbie Hoffman, in case you don't know, was one of the most prominent figures of the Flower Power Revolution which young people in the 1960s attempted against bourgeois society. I'm going to read you what he has to say about demonstrations."

He read from his notes, adding his own comments in places and, when the meeting ended, I picked up the sheets of paper. Here is what was on them:

Demonstrations always will be an important form of protest. The structure can vary from a rally or teach-in to a massive civil disobedience such as the confronting of the war-makers at the Pentagon or a smoke-in. A demonstration is different from other forms of warfare because it invites people other than those planning the action via publicity to participate. It also is basically non-violent in nature. A complete understanding of the use of media is necessary to create the publicity needed to get the word out. Numbers of people are only one of the many factors in an effective demonstration. The timing, choice of target and tactics to be employed are equally important. There have been demonstrations of 400,000 that are hardly remembered and demonstrations of a few dozen that were remarkably effective. Often the critical element involved is the theatre. Those who say a demonstration should be concerned with education rather than theatre don't understand either and will never organize a successful demonstration, or for that matter, a successful revolution. Publicity includes everything from buttons and leaflets to press conferences. You should be in touch with the best artists you can locate to design the visual props. Posters can be silk screened very cheaply and people can be taught to do it in a very short time. Buttons have to be purchased. The cheapest are those printed directly on the metal. The paint rubs off after a while, but they are ideal for mass demonstrations. You can print 10,000 for about 250 dollars. Leaflets, like posters, should be well designed.

One way of getting publicity is to negotiate with the city for permits. Again, this raises political questions, but there is no doubt one reason for engaging in permit discussions is for added publicity.

The date, time and place of the demonstration all have to be chosen with skill. Know the projected weather reports. Pick a time and day of the week that are convenient to most people. Make sure the place itself adds some meaning to the message. Don't have a demonstration just because that's the way it's always been done. It is only one type of weapon and should be used as such. On the other hand, don't dismiss demonstrations because they have always turned out boring. You and your group can plan a demonstration within the demonstration more accurately. Also don't tend to dismiss demonstrations outright because the repression is too great. During World War II the Danes held street demonstrations against the Nazis who occupied their country. Even today there are public demonstrations against the Vietnam War in downtown Saigon. Repression is there, but overestimating it is more a tactical blunder than the reverse. Nonetheless, it's wise to go to all demonstrations prepared for a vamping by the pigs.

After reading this, Shargunov put his notes aside and reminded us of the aims of Hurrah! "Our ideology is a synthesis of civil liberties, social welfare and a strong state. Our demonstrations are audacious street protests, ideological work, intellectual forums, recitals, manifestations of support from creative people, and promoting the interests of Russia and our population at the legislative level. Our plan is to become the government. Our motto is, 'We shall fight despite the flack!'"

"Morning! Motherland! Attack!" chanted youthful throats around me.

"We will fight despite the flack!" Shargunov repeated rather more loudly.

"Morning! Motherland! Attack!" the kids yelled, responding to his cue.

A head looked in anxiously at the door, ascertained there was no cause for concern, and withdrew.

Sergey explained the concept behind a demonstration scheduled for the middle of the next week, gave his helpers their instructions, and declared the meeting closed.

I didn't tell him that day about my plans. After the meeting a select few of us went to a cafe where we talked about everything except what was really on my mind. What, after all, was there to say when nothing was yet in place? If I had come straight out with my proposal for a revolutionary invasion of Turkmenistan, I doubt anyone would have reacted positively. They would more likely have decided I had a screw loose. I needed to go back home to work, or rather, to be in time to note down the revelations I had no doubt would again be vouchsafed me.

For someone to be willing to accept the terms of a new destiny you are proposing, they need at least to understand what fulfilment it can bring them, and what it is you are sending them out to die for.

16

> *"If you're so clever, why aren't you rich?"*
> American saying

From the windows of our apartment you can see the metal carcase of the "Moscow City" business complex under construction. The setting sun is reflected in its impersonal glazed windows and casts a pleasing glow.

People, hundreds of companies, will work in this modern building. Numerous workers will rush each day to their appointed workplace. They will, in all probability, feel they are the masters of the world as they look down from their glassy eminence on the lives of other people not fortunate enough to be in their place.

Each month, these souls will get their rubles in new white envelopes, fresh from their packaging and emblazoned, most likely, with the livery of some powerful corporation. With that money they will buy the things they need. What are these?

They will probably buy package holidays in Goa or the Maldives or somewhere else. The all-inclusive deal will cosset them comprehensively. The sea will relax their un-exercised bodies, lap at their atrophied muscles, and stir their souls into dreaming a little. When they come home, tanned and rested and with a special kind of good looks, they will tell their friends and colleagues what a great holiday they had. They will recommend a hotel they found, a particular tour operator and so on. They will share their new impressions.

They will be able to buy high-definition TVs, intriguing computers with surprisingly powerful processors, and match their mobile phones to the colour of their clothes. They will buy everything that can be bought, yet still aspire to something more. If they have an apartment, they will want a house. If they have a car, they will want a yacht. If they have a wife, they will want a mistress.

They will substitute money for God and the sense and meaning of life. Somebody once said that to be able to despise wealth, you need first to have it. I despise it while making do with poverty. There is something clean and neat and genuine about poverty, which is not always the case with wealth.

I wrote above, at the beginning of this tale, that I dream of that world of luxury and it is only because I can't have it that I follow a different way and reject theirs. Well now, my friends, that is no longer altogether true. It was. I was forever looking at expensive cars, people with bulging wallets, dressed to kill. I saw their photos on the Internet and wanted to belong with them. Okay, I was desperate for it and cried in the night because I couldn't have it now, today, not when I'm forty and burdened with a couple of kids and a flabby belly. Now, however, everything has changed. Now I am committed to my cause. I want to finish this book. I want to leave it like a scroll, like a portrait of my time, like a graphic image, for coming generations, of my struggle. I want by my definitive act to inscribe a magnificent full stop and walk off into eternity, to a place where I shall be master of the situation and where they, with all their money, will be unable to buy themselves the slightest chance of approaching me.

Am I sick? Perhaps. But I believe that all great men and women have been sick in one way or another and that it is nevertheless people like them, people like me, who move the world forward. It is we who direct the energies of ordinary people into a meaningful channel; even if our rebellion fails, as I sense that it will.

It will fail only in that we will fail to overthrow the regime, but in the sense in which I have conceived it, it will assuredly succeed. Our movement will live on after our deaths. Indeed, we may say it is only on that day that it will be born. Throughout the world the breeze will tug at our black and red flag. But first things first.

If the world were more receptive towards people like me, I would never have formulated my mission. Many people may already have forgotten a South Korean student called Seung-Hui Cho who carried out a massacre at Virginia Polytechnic Institute. Let me remind you. This twenty-three-year-old killed thirty-two people, wounded thirty and then put a bullet in his own head.

First he killed a girl he fancied and a student assistant. When he had done that, Cho went to a post office and mailed a DVD to the American NBC TV channel explaining his subsequent actions, and photographs in which he posed with weapons. In the video he said, "I did it. I had to ..." and added, "You had a hundred billion chances and ways to have avoided today. The decision was yours. Now you have blood on your hands that will never wash off."

I say the same to you, gentlemen. You too are implicated in everything that I am now doing. I felt our mutual antagonism particularly keenly at a concert by a certain rock group. Before the concert began, in a rather crowded bar, a great number of people with glasses of effervescent champagne were chatting, meeting up, kissing. They were in a world cut off from and inimical to me as I stood there by the wall in my sad white shirt and black trousers, clutching my jacket because there hadn't been a space for it in the cloakroom.

There was nobody on my side in that little skirmish. The mass of humanity confronting me, without even knowing it, humiliated and crushed me with its worldly knowledgeability. For a long time afterwards I remembered standing by that wall. I thought of it as my Wailing Wall.

Then those fine ladies and gentlemen went upstairs to the dress circle to the seats awaiting them, while I and others who seemed to be the same as me, although in outlook they belonged to the other side, went to stand at the front.

I was upset that night. I could feel a treacherous sweat breaking out on my back. I stared into the darkness of the dress circle. People were leaning over to whisper in the ears of their intimates. The performer was singing for them too. His eyes, his lips, the sounds of his song were directed to them, over my head.

I was standing, humiliated by my anonymity, at bottom right of the stage and the power of the amplifiers throbbed in my chest. I knew I was better than many of them there, one of the best. I did not doubt myself, any more than I doubted that I was just as deserving of smiles, champagne, and intimate whisperings in my ear.

I pictured myself as a rich businessman, or a successful writer, or the president, entering from behind glass doors obligingly opened for me by an attendant. I would be holding a leather suitcase, my shirt cuff casually but stylishly (as always with the rich) revealing a cufflink with an exquisite jewel. Well fitting, stout black patent-leather shoes would encase my feet, making me walk in a brisk, business-like manner. A mobile phone of precious metals would nestle in my pocket. I am walking arm in arm with Her (preferably a brunette slightly shorter than me, with gleaming white teeth continually revealed in a dazzling smile proclaiming her joy and admiration for me, the famous writer, or businessman or whatever, my sense of humour, my tact, my good manners and elegance). A shawl is draped over her shoulders and diamonds sanctify her ears.

We get into a dark stretch limousine with a driver in a peaked cap. "Drive on," I say and we glide off to the casino or my dacha or to visit some other personage as famous as me. We go anywhere you like, just as long as it's in that world which is closed to me now.

Did you notice the way I walked from the doors to the car? No limp. Instead I stepped out with the assured, smooth deportment of a confident male at one with the world and himself.

A talented hip-hop performer, Timati, came to that concert. He's big on the scene, owns clubs and restaurants and this whole hot world. He showed up with his trousers pulled down so you could see his underpants. He had his hands in his pockets, massive shades covering his eyes, just him and his buddy Pashu and some lady. They came and stood very close to where I was standing so forlorn and lonely to the right of the stage.

Somebody in front of them did not want to move back to let them see better. Pashu quickly sorted them out and they skulked off with their tail between their legs. I remember I so wanted to go up to Timati and say something I wouldn't normally dream of saying, like, "Bro, I know you're a busy man, but would you mind taking a look at my short stories? I've been writing for some time now but haven't made a penny. You can see, I'm young, I want cars, money, the high life." Or more simply, "Hi, guy! Tell me, how do I get to be like you?" No, that does not sound right. I just want to take from the world what belongs to me, yes, me, Artur Kara, someone who is not like anybody else.

While I was trying to come up with the right line, Timati and his friends headed for the exit. I stood for a moment, trying to tell myself that was fine, it didn't matter, but I lost the argument with myself and ran after them. There was no sign of them in the hall where, before the concert, I had been pinned to the wall by my obscurity. I rushed to the elevator, took it down and ran out into the wintry cold, just in time to see an orange Porsche drive off into the night. I didn't go back to the concert. Instead I went straight back home. I sat in the Metro trying not to cry, dejected, crushed.

That night I tossed and turned in a sweat, with tears in my eyes. I soaked the bedclothes in the course of that troubled night. I was handsome, strong and talented, and nobody wanted to know. Nobody cared. Was it my fault I wasn't born into a wealthy family but instead was the son of an ordinary mechanic? Did I stand condemned for that?

Assuredly, some writers had praised my work, but I had never won any of the competitions to which I submitted work and couldn't understand why. I wrote hundreds of letters to hundreds of magazines, mailed my work to them in large envelopes, by fax and e-mail. I did everything I could but nobody responded. Nobody could see me. Nobody could be bothered even to notice me.

When I did get an editor with his back to the wall as a result of my pestering, he might say a piece was quite well written and the theme was okay, only it didn't fit their profile. If he even said that. I included my phone numbers in every letter, mobile, landline, but the phones stayed silent. I didn't forget to give my address. I didn't know what to do next.

Meanwhile, hundreds of thousands of books which, to my way of thinking, were without merit, were being churned out. The top literary magazines were publishing works which provoked no emotional response. In order to fight the enemy you need to study him thoroughly, and I threw myself into doing just that. I read their books, I read and re-read their short stories and novellas in the magazines, and I just could not see what it was their work had that mine lacked.

And then, by chance, I had something published in an obscure magazine which had perhaps ten readers in all the world. How much that meant to me! I was sure that was it. I had successfully taken the first step and now, after this triumph, could look forward to hundreds, if not thousands, of publications.

How wrong I was! No matter that now I could add in my letters, "Several of my stories were published in the March issue of the prestigious literary magazine *Yunost*". This failed to produce the requisite effect and publishers continued to studiously ignore me. But that interval between my stories being accepted and the issue actually appearing was a magical time. I was so excited, eagerly anticipating my debut! My head full of dreams of future success, I worked every day. Still the magazine did not appear. I contained my impatience.

Eventually, it was due to hit the streets any day and again I sat up all night working. God knows, I did a huge amount of work! You claim there is justice in your world, but if so, why am I not rich?

I can only repeat the words of Seung-Hui Cho: "Guys, you had a billion chances to avoid this. The decision was yours. Now you have blood on your hands that will never wash off."

17

I was lying in bed in my room with the blinds blocking all daylight when it happened again. Letters, letters of fire, crimson, iridescent with all the colours of the rainbow, dazzling, a fireball of information suspended in the middle of my room. (I hope you're not getting tired of this.)

This time, the letters flying into my mind were accompanied by a man's voice. The sound was coming from inside my head, not outside, as would be more usual. Speaking in an even tone, he said:

"We shall call this new social and political movement 'Sense', and base it on The Revolutionary's Catechism by Sergey Nechayev. This pamphlet will make clear to your supporters the kind of behaviour you require from them. It will enslave the will of those who are most sincere and make them malleable. The Catechism was revealed to Nechayev just as it is being revealed to you, so it can be considered a universally applicable document, as you will come to see. Now, write!"

I quickly grabbed a ballpoint pen, an exercise book I found near at hand, and began writing.

"The Revolutionary's Catechism," the voice dictated the title. "For your information, I should mention that it was revealed and published as long ago as 1869. This young fellow, Sergey, was a lot like you. You would have found a common language and been friends, I am sure. A creator of destruction ... but that is for another time."

Calmly, unhurriedly, he read me the whole document from the airborne letters. It was like a light show and I was transfixed. I felt a chill of fear in the pit of my stomach but I was fascinated. I would have been hard pressed to think all this out on my own at twenty years of age. But whose voice was I hearing? Was it the voice of an angel or a demon? There was no telling.

I noted down this brutal manifesto, which seemed to undermine all good, humane feelings. It was, however, just what I needed and would bring me to my ineluctable end. I wrote it down gratefully.

The manifesto consisted of twenty-six points and was divided into four sections which considered the revolutionary's attitude towards himself, towards his revolutionary comrades, and towards society; and also the attitude soldiers of the revolution should adopt towards the common people.

I was commanded to edit some things and change others as I deemed fit, but overall, when reading the document later, I concluded there was almost nothing needing to be changed. It was 99.9% appropriate to my mission, ideally suited to it.

When we finished, the ball of light went out but the voice continued its declamation inside my skull. "That takes care of the rules for your fighters, Artur, but now you need to add a little in your own voice, so to speak. Something steeped in your own spirit, your own emotions. Something that will rally people to your banner rather than to others. Something that will get them marching behind you and willing to die for you. I've knocked some bits and pieces together. You'll find them in the third drawer of your desk. Use them.

"But that's for later. What we need right now is to get the banner sorted. If you are asked why it is needed and so forth, tell them that already as a child you understood the great psychological significance such symbols have and how they act primarily on the emotions. Tell them how one day after school you happened to see a mass protest in Mayakovsky Square. Tell them about that March of the Dissenters you were present at. Tell them that the sea of red banners, red armbands and red flowers was a compelling sight and you witnessed there the powerful impression a magical spectacle makes on uneducated people.

"The flag needs to express the ideas central to our movement, Sense, but at the same time it is crucial for its design to be expressive and attractive so that it affects the masses. You will come into close contact with the masses, and see how important even very small things are. A well-chosen party logo may be the first jolt arousing the interest of hundreds of thousands of people in the new movement. That, though, is all in the future. Right now you need to attract your first couple of hundred supporters."

"What will it be like later, after it's all over?" I couldn't help blurting out. "Afterwards, the movement will mushroom. It will take on a life of its own. Someone will appear to pick up your blood-stained banners and carry them forward over the chaos of life without sense or meaning. But let's get back to the flag.

"I have chosen black as the flag's main colour. As uncompromisingly dark as a moonless night, it will stand for the idea of Jihad, holy war against the infidels. Henceforth we shall define infidels not in terms of their belonging to a particular religion. That is outdated. When we speak of infidels we shall mean all who have turned away from the true meaning of existence, all who have chosen to barter their lives for worldly goods, disdaining the great sense of purpose they were born with.

"In the centre of a black background there will be a white circle, suggesting an authoritarian state with a strong leader, without which in the current situation it is impossible to construct any halfways meaningful society. White also stands for light and purity and elite status.

"Inside that white circle we shall place a red anemone. Have you ever seen an anemone?" the voice enquired. I shook my head, taken aback by how deep all this was. "Anemone coronaria is a member of the buttercup family, closely related to the delphinium, clematis and peony. The botanical name 'Anemone' comes from the Greek *anemos*, which means 'wind'.

"In feng shui the red anemone symbolises sincerity. It will do the same on our flag, symbolizing the sincerity of our impulse. The anemone is a flower as delicate as your own soul and, I hope, the souls of your future followers.

"In addition, red stands for blood and fire. Let me remind you that a new and better society can be created only by purifying blood. The colour red immediately intensifies the impact of any flag.

"That's all for today. Now, act!"

I was dumbfounded by this revelation. My goal seemed closer than ever. Usually, deciding on symbols, devising regulations and writing documents takes years and years, but everything had come to me in no time.

I went to the window, parted the slats of the blind and looked out at the sky. Dark, billowing thunderclouds were coming closer, threatening me with jagged lightning, trying to intimidate me with thunder. The sky began weeping great heavy raindrops which rapped at the window, smashed against it and burst, streaming down helplessly.

I thought about my parents. What would they do when I was gone? What would I do myself? Probably look down at the world from those clouds or whatever lies beyond them. Drink from rivers of milk, recline under the shady trees of paradise.

Remembering the documents the voice had talked of, I opened the third drawer of my writing desk and found a black folder. I turned it over and saw in the middle, sure enough, a white circle with a red anemone. Beneath our symbol was embossed the word 'SENSE'.

I sat down at the desk and opened the folder. It

contained a neat stack of papers entitled "Outlines of the Future State". I began reading with great interest, but after the first words, the first lines and paragraphs, I understood that I was the only person who could possibly have written this. Someone with an invisible trowel had excavated my heart and placed it in this folder. This was no dry, lifeless, bureaucratic document: it had a soul, it created a picture, or if not that, then at least a vague outline. I was surprised. Of course I was, but of late I had been getting used to miracles.

Outlines of the Future State
Initiative 1. Reform of Heating Provision

In these bleak days, when a lump rises in one's throat, at a time when one longs to laugh, greyish-white steam from the drainage system spreads out above the asphalt. The steam makes pathways for itself through an iron grid in the belly of grass which in places is piled high with dirty snow. In the vicinity of this grid it is somehow warm and cozy. There is no smell, which is odd. Elsewhere in Moscow the cold is penetrating, chilling everyone to the bone, but the grass around this grid is still green. The snow gets melted and irrigates the grass's roots with warm water. The soil around it is probably as warm as inside the houses. That is why there is no snow there and it is always warm, even in icy weather.

In view of this, I have concluded that we should change the heating system, initially in just one locality, on an experimental basis. If this succeeds, we can roll the system out in larger towns and then major cities.

The old heating stations must be destroyed and replaced by new facilities heated by human sewage. These waste products will be delivered to radiators which will warm apartments without the need for further heating. This will save the greater part of the energy used by existing installations and will have the following advantages:

1) no carbon footprint;

2) solution of the problem of heating in the coldest regions of Russia owing to the inexhaustible nature of the resource;

3) much cheaper maintenance costs of installations;

4) reduced demands on Russia's oil and gas reserves.

Finally, all citizens will be conscious of making a valuable contribution to the economy and will exert themselves to that end even more purposefully.

Outlines of the Future State

Initiative 2. Improvement of the Nation's Health

It has long been known that publicity campaigns intended to encourage people to adopt a healthy lifestyle have no effect on the crowds of dozy, pot-bellied men and tank-like women one sees when travelling on public transport. Why should they take any notice of them? They are perfectly content as they are. Repetitive work, meals three times a day, television, sleep. What else? Oh, I forgot the family (as these people themselves are gradually forgetting their families). They resign themselves to their family's existence and hand over their wages without any pleasure or the love they once felt.

Their babies grow into snotty kids before becoming traffic cops or mechanics like most of the rest of the Russian population. (Don't forget that Russia is not only Moscow and St Petersburg.) What progress is there? There is none, or at least little sense of it. A man has no money left over for educating his kids. It is difficult for a family of four to survive a month on, if he's lucky, 20,000 rubles. Food, clothing, outings (a rarity). The result is that a man leading this humdrum vegetative life loses heart. He becomes vacuous and fatuous. He does crosswords in the Metro. He is scared of the regime. He becomes obese.

Modern man has been deprived of the right to fight. He has been domesticated. The urge to fight, his rebelliousness, has been rooted out. The only place where a person can show aggression is when competing against other people on buses and trains. Here women too feel no inhibition about sweating, shoving other people aside with their corpulent bodies as they compete for a seat, and looking daggers at enemies who already have one.

I have not hitherto been involved in armed conflict, but saw the war in Chechnya on more than one occasion as a tourist. I have seen the ruined cities, the mangled cadavers of buildings. I have seen the jet fighters hurtling through the sky, the missiles they fire, felt the ground shake beneath my feet. I was not afraid. I smiled. I knew that people were dying, that grieving mothers' hearts were breaking, and yet I laughed as I brushed the dust from my face. This is better than docility. There is more life in war. War turns ordinary people into heroes.

And what about deportment! Have you noticed how people stoop? Round-shouldered, enslaved bodies. The solution cannot be just a matter of advertising a healthier lifestyle, displaying pumped-up, muscular bodies. You need tenacity to achieve that. You need to spend time and money (and most people, remember, are short of money).

Membership at a fitness centre costs around $1,000 a year, far more than most Russians can afford, and the popular view is that it is money down the drain. A modest set of exercises which can be done at home, like press-ups, pull-ups and sit-ups on a hard floor, are soon dismissed as too boring. The people demand results. They want a miracle and they want it now, or at least very soon. No one can promise results like that to some fatso, let alone instantly.

Lateral thinking suggests a different solution. Our legislators need to pass a law requring that people in public places and government institutions (offices, schools, the Duma, etc.) go naked.

Even if your body is less than perfect, you will soon notice that your back straightens of its own accord. Knowing that your belly flab is being seen not only by you but by everybody around you, you will immediately take steps on your own initiative to deal with it. All of Russia, an absolute majority of the population, will start doing exercises and will be the healthier for it, and better-looking, and prepared to work small miracles!

The president himself should be in the nude when he signs the act into law, in order to set an example to citizens. After all, he doesn't seem to have anything to be ashamed of, or does he?

Outlines of the Future State
Initiative 3. The Family

What is a family? What does the concept mean to each of us? Is it really the nucleus of society? (Criminal 'families' apart. I am using the word in its traditional sense.)

On page 711 of Ozhegov's Dictionary this social phenomenon is defined as follows:

1. A group of closely related people who live together;

2. An association of people united by common interests;

3. A group of animals or birds consisting of a male, a female and their progeny; also a separate group of animals, plants or fungi of the same species.

That's it. Not a squeak about a sacred, inviolable institution. To a layman the word 'family' is usually associated with the first definition.

If you ask the man in the street what a family is, he will most often reply, "Well ... a dad, a mum, a deaf grandfather, a grandmother, a sister – and all sorts of other relatives (although they aren't really your family, just your relatives)."

Teenagers, with their customary maximalism, pull a face at any mention of the family, while adults talk about it with indifference. If you turned off the sound, you might think they were answering a question about their favourite brand of beer. "Well, there's Melnik and, er, Bochkarev, Klin Pale, Kozel and, er... Bailey's – oh no, that's not a beer it's a liqueur."

That's how people think. The family today has no practical meaning. It is just a place where you belong, to which you can return any time, no matter what you have done. The family is a nest to which most people eventually stop coming back and go off to build one of their own.

The fledglings in a new nest grow up, leave it and make their own in accordance with a logic only nature understands. That is the life we are offered, stripped to its bare essentials. Oh, you also need to get worms and insects to bring home to the babies and for yourself. Childhood is a good time. Your parents bring you food and even put it in your beak.

It doesn't make much sense nowadays to talk about the second definition of 'family'. We can only read about families like that in old books. But for them, we would have casually deleted the definition as inapplicable.

We do not live in the eighteenth century, when families gathered in the evenings to knit, or in the nineteenth, when a blooming girl would sing an aria from a popular opera while accompanying herself on the pianoforte.

Nowadays that kind of display would be considered vulgar and someone would turn the TV up louder. For girls, singing is just a hobby. They can sing to themselves while drying their hair, they can sing the words of the latest hit in the shower, but no more than that. They shouldn't be looking for an audience. Reading in modern families is also not something that could provide a topic for discussion in the evening. Everyone reads what interests them and the definition 'an association of people united by common interests' no longer fits.

Of course, some families do have common interests. They work for generations at a particular profession, but they are a small minority. Even in these families, interests change. A moment eventually comes when a family member has had enough and rebels.

The idea of destroying the family is at present largely perceived as nonsense, because a clear majority of them remain together, underwritten by signatures on what looks like a contract of life-long cooperation and support. If, however, we destroy families systematically, en masse, but without denying people feelings of love for each other, without taking away the right to care for each other, we can build a qualitatively new society with a great deal more meaning.

We should not mulishly believe that the family is the cornerstone of everything. In the beginning there was nothing. When the first people appeared there were no families. Stories about Adam and Eve serve to reinforce people's belief that the family is a solution, a way to live life to some purpose. What needs to be remembered, however, is that what the common people think of as 'revelations from God', contained in thousands of books, of which the bestsellers are the Bible and the Q'uran, were written by human beings.

Many of you have come to recognize that the family is without meaning but often have not dared to say so. Anyway, what would be the point? I admit, the idea of losing the family is frightening, because our present society does not offer any substitute as stable as this institution which occupies such an important place in the present system of relationships. The state of which I write, and which I intend to create in the future, will renounce many prejudices, including the family. What do we want instead? I shall write about that later.

I will say only that the word 'family' will be replaced by 'commune'. To doubters, of whom there are many, I say that this future state is no mirage I have seen while suffering a lonely delirium, no phantasmal oasis in the desert, but a real, existing territory. Palm trees grow there. To the east its shores are washed by one of the great seas of the planet. It has a sub-tropical climate, with warm, dry summers and mild winters. It also has a desert, mountains and long rivers full of large fish. Deep beneath it are many natural resources. If we reduce its borders and find the necessary political will within ourselves, we can offer citizens the choice of not working and simply distribute income from its natural resources to the population at large.

I think of all this and am filled with energy. I understand the senselessness of everything around us, and it is just a pity that we need, nevertheless, to wade through it all.

Outlines of the Future State
Initiative 4. Education. What We Have

I went to "History of Religions" today. This subject, like many others taught at our Uni, just scrambles people's brains. The students, squirming on uncomfortable benches, reluctantly take notes, fuss over their mobile phones as if they were five-day-old babies, and play word games as if what is going on in the lecture hall is nothing to do with them. These are the 'normal' students, recognized as 'owning' the university and, more to the point, regarding themselves as normal.

This knowledge will have flown their docile heads by tomorrow, if not by this evening. It will have been squeezed out by, at best, an oriental language, or a TV reality show. "The most important postulates of Christianity ..." my unreceptive ears register. "Okay, this could be interesting," you think, but then it is spoiled by a long list of postulates: the mariological, the soteriological, the ecclesiological ("best reflected in the writings of Gregory Palama").

Who needs this stuff? Events will erode all useless knowledge but cannot return youth to you. They will not give you back the fresh emotions, the intense delight in a warm spring breeze which can be felt only by a seventeen-year-old beast with the countenance of an angel. Nothing will come back. Instead a paunch will come. Your breasts will hang limply just above your navel. Long johns and thermal underwear will enter your life and no longer shock you, as will armchairs with sagging seats whose red velvet upholstery has been worn away by your backside.

It is spring outside and somewhere happiness is sauntering. Am I weird? Perhaps you really are normal. Perhaps there's no need to ask unnecessary questions, to waste time on nonsense? No need to ask yourself and the world, "What's all this for?" Perhaps you should just learn what you are taught and not what interests you, accept the view that "It's the only way you're going to graduate from your Uni", which really does strike home.

I surreptitiously take in the lecture hall, crowded

almost to overflowing. I look at the lecturer who has been pontificating now for nearly fifty minutes. "NO!" my spirit shouts. "NO!" my body cries. "NO!" I yell with every fibre of my delicate being.

This is all beside the point, and the point is that you are unhappy! The point is that you have been browbeaten by parents, teachers, life, and God knows what else into accepting that this is as it should be!

"Study or you won't get anywhere!" you've had drummed into you since childhood. That is true of the world we live in today, but this is a world of slaves, faceless clerks and unhappy students. It is a world of divorces and orphans, a world of violence and pillaging, where presents replace love, where love is a present. No money – no honey.

This is a world where there is no place for me or for the best of you, for all who are not robots submitting to the spirit of the times but individuals with a sense of eternity who can feel, instinctively, that something is wrong.

There is a different world! There will be a different world!

"The Schism in the Church", "Pretenders during the period of the Arab Caliphate..." (one of them was a woman, believe it or not, I can't remember her name – she must have been wild.)

If G-d really existed (He does, for Christ's sake!), if He really needed and loved us, cherished us, if He had really tried to save the world, we wouldn't exist! Not as we are. We would be happy, every last one of us! There would be no despondency. Happiness and love and trust would have taken over the world.

That hungry, good-natured soul in tattered rags stretching out his hand in the church porch, a quintessential believer, would receive warm clothes and a crust of bread from heaven, yes, from heaven! He wouldn't need to beg from his 'neighbour'. What, after all, is he asking for? No more than that. He would be given a roof over his head if only God existed (and He does!) and if He cared about us. There would be no religions at all, just God performing miracles, strengthening our faith. Moses, Jesus, Muhammad are light-years away from me, I have no memory of them. I have never heard their voices, never seen their eyes. Did Buratino really exist? Did Pinocchio? People say they did, and books have been written and movies made about them.

We need a different world. I believe we are many. If we are to succeed in changing the world we need real strength. This is my cry in the wilderness of the Land of Senselessness.

I conjure you all! Now!

18

The next day I learned that my father was dead.

"Artur! Artur!" my mother shouted down the phone line. "Artur!" She kept calling my name. "Artur! He ... He ... Your father ..." She was choking on the words and I knew immediately that something irreparable had happened.

"I'll be right over!" I replied from the already familiar apartment at Chistye Prudy, to which I had brought the documents written for my new movement and the design for its logo but had not ventured to show them.

Heydar was in top form that day. I found two of his statements particularly memorable: one about the coming of the Mahdi, and the second about the meaning of time.

"As for the Mahdi (may Allah hasten his return)," he said. "We are required to understand that he cannot be an ordinary historical personage emerging out of the people of his time, even of those related to the family of the Prophet.

Such an interpretation could give rise to profanation or even sincere but sterile pretenders."

"What is the nature of the Mahdi?" a brusque, wiry man with a beard asked. His hand was shaking and the third finger was missing. "The Mahdi combines two natures," Heydar willingly replied. "He is a living individual like you or me, but at the same time exists outside the laws of time and space." "But where?" a chubby man in his mid-thirties and wearing a green skullcap asked. "The All-High protects him among us as a hidden presence until the hour when the sum of our efforts is sufficiently worthy for him to appear and lead us or our successors to the last times."

About the meaning of time, he said that "Nothing in our life is more valuable than the time which we have. That is why people exchange their time for money, for wealth, for pleasure, believing that is an advantageous exchange, a worthwhile "ajr". That is why God warns that it is in fact a very bad and erroneous bargain."

Without saying goodbye, putting on my boots as I left, I ran down to the street. I looked at a world in which everything had grown dim. Only now did I begin to register the gravity of what had happened. It was like a sledgehammer blow to my head which paralyzed me and brought thoughts as dark as the depths of a cave into my heart.

I had a long way to travel and time to think many things over. When I recalled memories of my childhood, I several times burst into tears which came faster than I could wipe them away. My whole being was suddenly filled with warmth but then I was gripped by a chilling sense of the irretrievable loss of something close and uniquely dear to me.

How many things I now longed to say to him! How many loving words which had been held back by the pincers of my oriental upbringing, which had no place for tenderness between men. These pincers released me now. They no longer made any sense, and left behind great, bleeding gashes. I was crying and soon my whole sleeve was wet with tears.

My movement, Sense, seemed now to make little sense. How he had wanted me to become a normal person! How many times he had warned me against my chosen path! Who knows, perhaps that had sapped his spirit and been the cause of his death.

It may be that God, or whoever is up there in the heavens disposing our destinies, decided to take him to himself in order to send me forth on my personal journey, so that no one of importance to me should gainsay my will.

When I reached home my Dad's Lada-9 was sitting mangled in the courtyard. The saloon looked as if it had been squeezed by two huge hands with superhuman strength which had tried to play the car like a concertina.

I learned afterwards that the accident happened as he was driving home, very near our block. The tow truck, not knowing what to do with this lump of unwanted scrap, brought it back to our yard. Dad wasn't killed outright. Bleeding and with multiple fractures, he overcame the pain and, finally managing to stop a taxi, struggled back to his place in the beehive.

There were drops of blood in the elevator. I came up to the ninth floor, trying to swallow down the lump stuck in my throat. It wouldn't go away. Instead it grew inexorably, choking me. Tears again began to run down my face. I glimpsed my fine head with its crew cut, my aquiline nose. It must have been the emotional disturbance, but I thought I looked really handsome.

The door handle was ringed with dried blood. There was blood on the hallway floor, shouting and women wailing. My mother ran to me and for a moment I didn't recognize her. Her face haggard, her eyes wet, she had aged decades. She seemed to have been hammered down by the misfortune to half her former size.

She started wailing again and threw her arms round me. "My son, my son! Don't go in there, son! Don't look!" Tears flowed from my eyes and wet the head of the woman who gave me life, as trustingly she laid her head on my chest.

I could do nothing to relieve the anguish of this woman so close to me. No more could Limonov, Jemal or Shargunov, let alone those founding documents of Sense which had appeared from nowhere. Nobody in this world could help her, nobody! Only my father, and he no longer existed. Only the man who had stood between her and the world, who had become her world. Now her world was at an end. It had dissolved, washed away by her tears.

I knew that perfectly well, but nevertheless tried automatically to console my inconsolable mother. "Never mind," I kept saying, though what that was supposed to mean I had no idea. I could give her no comfort either through my talent or my mission, through my condoling, my bedsheet in a museum or my serene ceiling. Only he could have, an ordinary engineer who had spent his life performing simple, monotonous tasks but who had some focal point in his heart, some inner system of coordinates which was now lost forever, and which had not been passed on to me.

My mother suddenly pulled back from me and fixed her strong, wrinkled hands in a vice-like grip on my shoulders. A malign, probably crazed, look gleamed in her eyes, a look of reproach which chilled me to the bone.

"It's all your fault!" she cried, not for an instant believing her own words. She said it again: "It's all your fault!" She resigned herself to the idea and began pummeling me with her fists. "It's you, you wretch, you fool! It's all your fault my Islam is dead! Because of you! You have stolen his life! You reptile! You pig! You are not my son!" She thumped away at me as hard as she could and it seemed to be helping her. "How many times did he tell you? Plead with you? How many times? But would you listen? Ever since that argument at the dinner table he wasn't the same! His only son!" she said contemptuously. "His only son had turned out to be a complete wastrel! To defy your father like that!"

"From the very beginning we dreamed, from the very beginning ..." Her blows were becoming weaker. "We dreamed that our son, our little ray of sunshine, our Arturchik would become a diplomat, a lawyer, perhaps a doctor! How your father longed for that." Another blow, really no more than a poke. "How he wanted you to go further than he had been able to, to really become someone ... And I ... That's what I wanted too ... But you ..."

Her face pale, her dull eyes those of someone whose life has lost its meaning, she almost collapsed. Her legs gave way but I caught her. As limp as a second-hand dress on a hanger, her weak arms clung to me while I dragged her to a chair.

"Oh, son, my little boy, forgive me! You're the only person I have left! You and your sister ... but she'll be off and married before you know it ... It's just you, my little sunshine. You are all I have left. Your father has left me and my daughter will too. Only you, please do not go away! Stay with me ... I beg you ...." I brought her a glass of water.

It was very strange. Everything that was happening, in spite of all my emotions and inner turmoil, seemed like a movie which ought to be about to end, or a dream I would wake from in a sticky sweat and have forgotten by tomorrow. Except that the movie wasn't ending. I shook my head and didn't manage to wake up either.

I simply refused to believe what had happened. Yes, the wrecked car was down in the yard. Yes there was blood all over the apartment. I could see a trail of it leading to the far room from which I could hear my sister's moans. Yes, there was my wraith-like, grief-stricken mother in front of me.

It all just seemed too simple. A person was alive. He lived and was purposeful. The years passed and he went forward in life, maybe quickly, maybe slowly, but he went forward. He worked at his job, brought up his children, and then smack! Wallop! That's it. The End. You no longer exist on this Earth.

I went in the direction of the moaning. In the middle of the room, on an old red carpet lay my father. I couldn't see his face. Madina had her head on his chest. Her disheveled hair was stuck together in braids by blood, glued together by this testimony of death.

In the end, hearing my footsteps, she raised her head and I could see everything. A realization as bright as a flash of lightning told me I no longer had a father.

19

It was decided my father should be taken back to Chechnya in the car of his cousin from Lyublino. He would be buried there in the family cemetery, next to his father and mother. They would wrap him in a shroud, align him with the East, and place a slab over him with Arabic script on the sides.

There wasn't enough room in the car for me so I had to stay in Moscow. To tell the truth, that suited me fine. I felt a brief period of solitude could only be helpful.

The apartment was thoroughly cleaned to remove

all trace of the recent occurrence. Dad's car was taken off to the scrapyard and everything returned to normal, except that every so often my heart would miss a beat and remind me of some episode in our family life.

Here was Dad sitting watching the television with us. There were the buttons on the remote control, almost erased where he had pressed them. There was the chair he used to sit in, and so on. Everything still bore the imprint of his presence. These thoughts would not leave me in peace.

What if I was wrong! What if my mission was just a figment of the overheated imagination of a disaffected teenager? Actually I was twenty, just about to turn twenty-one, and still completely unknown.

However dear my childhood memories and my warm and touching relationship with my parents, I forced myself to despise them now. The senseless existence of the mother who had brought me up and now didn't know what to do with herself; the senseless life and equally absurd death of my father! I came into serious conflict with myself and spent hours lying on my bed, propping up the ceiling with the intensity of my stare, despairing of being able to overcome those tender but surprisingly well-rooted shoots of goodness sown in me in my childhood. I needed to root out any compassion I might feel for others, rid myself of it once and for all, hurl it far away from my self.

Quite separate from this conflict, but in close proximity, a second struggle was taking place, no less fierce than the first but with a longer history. "Perhaps you should just stop." A cold, metallic voice plunged into me like a stone thrown into a deep, dark well and unable to find the bottom. In one way or another I had brought about the death of one person, and now I was preparing to send to their deaths perhaps another hundred.

I did not doubt that hundreds of people would follow me, rallying to that inspiring banner. What did hundreds matter when in the world there are billions? I needed just a couple of hundred brave, underprivileged boys and girls, unable to make their way in life and who wanted to die heroically.

I knew Nazir Magomedov and Akhmad Zherebin would bring some along; some would be provided by Heydar Jemal, some by Sergey Shargunov. That was where the handful of heroes would come from who would make these lines I am writing infinitely precious.

I had all the cards in my hand. I had a pretext, to subvert an unconstitutional state system which had incarcerated in its torture chambers revolutionaries of whose glorious deeds I shall write below. I had at my disposal ideas for building a fundamentally new society which would destroy the tried and trusted but partly obsolete mechanisms of social, political, ethical etc etc life. I had The Revolutionary's Catechism which laid down what I required of my adherents. I had in my hands the staff bearing the billowing standard of Sense. I had a charismatic leader: myself. And I had the guts to do all this. At least I hoped I had.

The only thing bothering me was the absence of any meaningful love interest in my story. There wasn't much I could do about that. I was lame, almost disabled, and poor into the bargain. I was in pursuit of an absolute beauty so far beyond my reach as to be unattainable. I had no wish to limp my way for a lifetime through the pathetic existence on offer.

Of course, if I were to direct my energy not into destroying but into creating, if I were to direct it into a peaceful channel I was quite sure I could become someone, a banker, a businessman or a lawyer. In order to do that, however, I would have to play by their rules. Study, work for years, get drunk on Fridays at corporate bonding sessions. Wait, wait, wait! Well, I couldn't wait. Life had tasked me with solving all my problems fast. I had no time to spare for wearing out the seats of numerous pairs of trousers in a succession of offices.

If normal people aspire to build on society as it already exists, "so that future generations should have a better life", I wanted to demolish this world right down to its foundations, leaving only scorched earth. I wanted to eradicate rule by the majority with all their terms and conditions so that in the future people like me should have the opportunity to build a new society.

I was fully aware that I would not succeed in scorching the Earth. I knew our rebellion would drown in its own blood, but I wanted to set an example. With the dedication of a samurai, I honed the harakiri knife to show the world that I had not been vanquished by you lot with all your pseudo-knowledge and pseudo-qualifications. In unheroic times I chose to die a hero.

Do you know how I pictured that to myself? Nowadays we have a machine called a car. It is crammed with all manner of technological wizardry, designer gear and God knows what else. Generations of people have squandered their lives, toiling to create this machine. Someone perfected the engine, someone invented the colour display, someone designed the supremely comfortable seats. Then someone else broke his back to get the money to buy this car and finally succeeded. Now it's my turn. I am the one who smashes the window with a heavy bat, gets inside and, jamming the accelerator down to the floor, takes off towards the distant horizon and a better life.

I decided to post Outlines of the Future State as a series of articles on the Internet in order to attract supporters. I phoned Nazir and Akhmad, Heydar Jemal and Sergey Shargunov, and invited them all to a meeting in a little-known cafe. I told them it was very important, a matter of life and death, and that they absolutely must clear their calendars and get there by seven o'clock that evening.

It has been raining for days. People sheltered under umbrellas and skipped around, trying to avoid puddles and the rivulets of water flowing along the edges of the roads. Menacing thunderclouds hung over the city and it seemed nothing could dislodge them. Only blinding flashes of lightning sliced through their bodies and the thunder exploded them from inside like dynamite.

A violent wind bent the trees, possessing them like whores, slaking its desire. With a malicious grin it turned umbrellas inside out, buffeting people, piercing them like toys with needles of cold.

20

I stood in front of a mirror, examining my reflection. Today everything would be decided. These men would have to show their hand. Who would stay and who would leave would become known in just a couple of hours, but right now, I had time to prepare. What should I wear? This was a very important day, one of the most important in my life. Today I would finally know the names of those who would die with me for our cause.

I remember being vexed that I didn't have anything rescmbling a military uniform. I would have liked to wear the uniform of Sense, with its flag emblazoned on the breast, but as I had none, I put on an ordinary pair of black jeans, a black shirt, and my father's black leather military belt.

For a while I turned this way and that, examining myself in the mirror approvingly. Here am I, Artur Kara, great writer and rebel leader, founder of Sense, man of destiny. Sharp, piercing eyes, strong cheekbones, fetching crew cut. I ran a hand over it and was satisfied with the prickliness of every hair. They felt like bayonets ready for the fray, bayonets pointed skywards before the taking of the stronghold.

I raised my arms and tensed them, making the biceps bulge. It has to be said that, since I really got into all this, I had changed beyond recognition. Daily work-outs at home had produced results. I pulled my shirt up to my chest. Muscles now covered my body like a coat of armour sculpted by a jeweller.

I was ready in every sense for this campaign. I even said to myself that day, "If they all deny me, if they mock me I shall not deviate from my path!"

I jabbed my index finger at the mirror. "Is that clear? I shall never deviate from my path!" Already on my way out the door, I looked back and said straight into the mirror, "No matter what the cost!"

I walked down the stairs to warm up, to exercise my muscles before the battle, the way boxers warm up before a fight. I had no car waiting for me because, as you will remember, despite my status, I didn't possess one. Instead, in the breast pocket of my shirt, I carried two season tickets: a soft one with a magnetic strip for overground transport, and a thick card one with a black-and-white photograph of the holder for travel on the Metro.

In my hands I carried the folder which I had so surprisingly found in the third drawer of my desk, with the vivid symbol of Sense, a red anemone inside a white circle on the folder's black cover. "Anemone for sincerity," went round and round in my head as I walked to the bus stop. "Sincerity. A symbol of the purity of our aspirations. *Anemos* – the wind. The wind! The wind!"

Gusts of wind tried to blow me heavenwards before I had completed my earthly mission. The rain, taking the forecasters by surprise, had lasted for several days before just as suddenly stopping. Now, at first timidly, then more and more assertively, it was again taking possession of the land, cleansing the territory around me. I never did know what it was the rain wanted to tell me. Perhaps to warn me? That will forever remain a mystery.

Passing through the yellow turnstile by the front door of the trolleybus, I moved down inside. At first I took up a position by the wide rear window, resting my arms on the conveniently placed rail, but after a few stops decided to sit. The black leatherette seat gasped despairingly under the pressure of my body. I leaned my head on the cool glass. From the other side, raindrops crashed into it and burst open.

At first I imagined they were trying to assassinate me, to raindrop me to death, and that only the shatterproof window of the trolleybus was saving me, but then I asked myself why the heavens would want to kill me. They were on my side and, despite the voluntary nature of my actions, I was in effect acting on their instructions. I decided the heavens were lamenting me, their earthly champion, and perked up.

Opening the folder, I considered the documents in my armoury. The uncompromising twenty-six points of The Revolutionary's Catechism looked up at me, and my Outlines of the Future State about which, for some reason, I felt a little embarrassed. Probably because it was the first political manifesto I had written, the fruit of my own lengthy deliberations.

Of course, it was not a comprehensive collection of the documents needed to transform the world, or indeed even the particular country I had chosen, but as a means of shaking the ground beneath the feet of a handful of individuals it fitted the bill very well.

I was browsing through the last pages of Outlines, where I was criticizing the present education system, when I realized this was by no means the last document, although I distinctly remembered that I had packed only that and the Catechism, which I had hastily printed out from my notes. As I turned the last page of the documents I knew about, a chill ran down my spine.

"An Attempt to Seize Power", ran the headline. I started reading the report, but was barely a quarter of the way through it when I stopped, conscious of someone staring at me intently. You've probably had a similar feeling when you're absolutely sure someone is watching you, although you haven't yet spotted who.

I looked up casually and turned round. A man sitting across the aisle to my left had his back against the window, his foot brazenly on the seat next to him, and continued staring at me, not fazed in the slightest by being detected. I looked down at the closed folder and up again. He had not gone away. There he sat, and I thought he winked his left eye at me. I took a closer look. He had a scrawny ginger beard, tufts of unkempt hair, and black circles under his fingernails. He looked a complete deadbeat. Large plastic bags by his feet were stuffed with goods of some description.

"I wonder what he's after?" I remember thinking. "Perhaps he's a psycho?" I'm not scared of psychos. I could easily hold my own against them, or so I thought, but to be reduced to this guy's sex object I found demeaning. I lowered my eyes again, deciding that if he was still gawping at me when I looked up I would move to the front of the bus. I didn't want to soil my hands on him on such a momentous day.

The bum was still watching and in his drunken blue eyes as crystal clear as spring water, I saw something like knowingness. Don't ask why I thought that, I just did. In his smirk there was something that neutralised me, so stressed out over my imminent fateful meeting.

I was just about to get up and move, as I had decided, when I had to sit straight back down again. Now it was not the bum sitting there but Sergey Zverev, Moscow's renowned style icon, immaculate in a snowy white suit, a hat slightly tilted, and with a shaggy lilac-coloured wrap, which might have been fur for all I know, draped over his shoulders. Zverev's legs were sheathed in tall, black leather boots with high platform soles. He was looking out the window, but his prominent lips, lavish with pink lip gloss, were parted in exactly the same smirk. I could not believe my eyes. I didn't shut them because that never changes anything, so I just stared fixedly out my window.

Suddenly I heard, "Oh, it's the great Artur Kara! This celebrity's in shock!" Zverev was standing in the aisle, gazing at me. "Why didn't I recognize you! Listen, have you got a mirror?"

"What? Oh, no," I mumbled abashed.

"Bother! I left my bag in the car. How could I know I'd have to whizz around in a trolleybus? Oh well, never mind." So saying, Zverev noticed a large window in which, because of the lighting in the bus and whatever, he could see his reflection, if only dimly.

With one leg straight and the other slightly to one side, placing his right hand on his chest and with the other toying with his wrap, he addressed the world in general,

"Which lucky person is going to get such beauty!" He added, "This celebrity's in shock!"

I was surprised no less than the celebrity standing in front of me on his high platform boots inside a moving trolleybus.

"Next stop, Metro station ..." The announcement caught me by surprise and I headed belatedly for the exit.

"Good luck out there, Artur! Incidentally, about the hair. Drop by soon, we'll buff up that image of yours," Zverev called after me and, making a pretence of licking his finger, slicked his eyebrow. "I'd usually charge 5,000 rubles just for that, but knowing your situation we'll fix you up for free."

"Thanks," was as much as I had time to reply because someone was shoving me in the back. I thought it must be some old granny and made haste to get out in order to avoid an earful of coarse abuse, but the voice of a young woman surpassed all expectations.

"Move, will you, infernal bollockhead!"

I got off the bus and looked round. TV personality Ksenia Sobchak, wearing a skimpy translucent dress, looked back at me.

"What are you staring at?" she demanded, before suddenly stopping short. "Oh, Artur, I'm sorry. Excuse me, for heaven's sake. I didn't recognize you. I feel a complete idiot," she said, fanning herself with her hands as if wafting a blush of embarrassment from her face. "It's just, well you know, you come across all sorts of people on public transport."

I hurried away, from the bum with the clear blue eyes, from the fashion stylist who replaced him, from the abusive society lioness, and soon the Metro was whisking me away from these to other events, to my meeting with the men I had decided to entrust with my secret. What were these people doing in a trolleybus and how did they know me?

The bum with his knowing grin, Zverev's strange smile, Sobchak in her best frock? It seemed to make no sense.

I tried to rid myself of these thoughts and focus on the business in hand, but couldn't. Those words, "This celebrity's in shock!" and "Infernal bollockhead!" pursued me, constantly re-surfacing in my mind. The people around were perfectly ordinary. Those who had managed to bag a seat were dozing peacefully, or reading newspapers and books. I wondered whether they would read my words the same way. What would they have to say about me?

Does it matter? Oddly enough, it really did matter to me. I was probably an exhibitionist. Scornful of public opinion in my own life, I was nevertheless worried about what people would say when I was gone. How would they rate my campaign? That fat lady there, for instance. Would the event unsettle her, or would she placidly switch to a different channel, not turning a hair as the newsreader said, "It has been announced that the leader of the Sensites ..."? I did not and could not know, so I decided the thing to do was to act according to the dictates of my heart and think no more about my future reputation.

It was of no interest to me how inspired these generations of the 1960s or 70s had been. I was not planning to dance a jig on their graves, any more than I was planning to preach a sermon about our 'lost generation' and the death of idealism. That was not what mattered to me. Other people concerned themselves with all that now, and more would in the future. I just wanted to get on with my mission, in full awareness of the likely outcome. I was preparing to go into battle.

I carried on reading the papers in my folder from the point where I left off in the bus and was amazed. I imagine you, like me, have a fair idea who put those additional papers in it. That might have deterred a less determined man. Before a bull will charge you, you have first to wave a red rag in front of its nose. In order to get a snake to bite, you need first to invade its territory.

21

We were all assembled, in a dimly lit windowless basement, at a grainy wooden table you could stick large knives into without causing serious damage. We greeted each other as brothers, but only I knew why I had brought them here today, or what I had meant when I spoke of a matter of life or death. I could see they were fairly quizzical, but willing to hear me out.

"Well now, Artur, I have had to put all my business on hold," Heydar said. "I hope there was good reason for me to do so."

"You need have no doubt of that," I answered confidently and, addressing all those present, went on, "Irrespective of the decision each of you personally takes, I guarantee that none of you will feel this day has been wasted. Each will have something to look back on in later life. First, though, perhaps we should order something."

Nazir and Akhmad-Pavel exchanged glances, Shargunov reached for the menu which was in a stand near him, and Heydar made no move. "I propose we have a large pot of jasmine tea and five mugs." I believed that drinking from the same teapot should symbolize our unity. "Is that agreeable?"

"Why jasmine?" Akhmad asked.

"Because the jasmine flower is a symbol of blamelessness, which is particularly appropriate to the topic we have to discuss," I elucidated.

"Agreed. I have no further questions," he said, raising

his hand to vote for the motion and with an unexpected smile on his usually unsmiling face.

Shargunov's gaze moved from one person to another, occasionally distracted by what was going on at adjacent tables.

I ordered jasmine tea for all of us and, when it was brought, poured it into the mugs of these comrades I was hoping to convert into supporters.

When each had taken a sip, I began. "Very well, let's make a start. I have asked you here today in order to announce that I have established Project Sense."

Regrettably but predictably I noticed wry smiles on the faces of my audience, and in my head heard Sergey Zverev's voice: "This Celebrity's in Shock!"

I pressed on. "Only, I would ask you not to be in too much of a hurry to interrupt, or sneer, or whatever. God knows I have been brought to this place by good intentions, and it is they which have led me to convene this gathering of people I believe to be honourable and noble.

"You have differing views, ideas and priorities in life. All of you, indeed, except Nazir and Akhmad, belong to different parties. Let that not deter you, because the ideology of the movement to be known as Sense will sweep those boundaries away. Its principles are universal and will appeal to every freedom-loving person.

"I am talking about freedom of death! The freedom of every individual to choose for himself a worthy end to his journey on this earth. Last week my father was killed," I said, offering them the story as an example, "in a car crash on his way home. He died in accordance with the inscrutable will of the Creator. All his plans and aspirations were brought low, his whole lifestyle negated by this tragedy. And now he lies in the earth."

"We will all die sooner or later," Nazir reflected.

"And then, since the Almighty is the creator of all earthly things, he has the right to take any of us whenever He sees fit," Heydar elaborated. "Our Prophet Muhammad, may Allah honour him and grant him peace, said, 'Always remember the destroyer of pleasures – death'."

The topic of death proved, as I had expected, to be close to the heart of every person I had invited. Akhmad had been listening attentively, Akhmad, our Pavel, who had searched for a new way in this life and finally found it in an explosive mixture of Islam and National Bolshevism, now commented meditatively, "There is no doubt that Almighty Allah has determined the span of life for all people. When that time comes, the messengers of the Lord gather up the soul of the slave of God without exception. Anyone who thinks about death realizes that this greatest event in human life is the lot of everyone. Wherever a person may be, no matter who he is, death comes to him and takes him from this world and into another world, where either Heaven or Hell await him." Then he asked, "So what can you propose?"

The four of them looked at me, wanting an answer. I could have gone into reverse gear, resorted to demagoguery to enhance their respect for me as a 'far-sighted politician', or at least I could have tried. Now would have been a good moment for winning these people over in that way, to line up our movement alongside all the others which lead a peaceful existence, to make contact with them, to sit at endless roundtables and hold conferences. I could have plunged head first into that world of papers and mineral water fizzing in tall cut glasses.

When a movement is still weak, it always faces the temptation of persuading itself that it is all right to stay with the majority for a time and 'sing from the same hymn sheet'.

At such moments, human cowardice looks so diligently for arguments in favour of that tactic that some can always be found to demonstrate what a great idea it is to support a criminal mass movement "with a view to forwarding our own interests".

I had thought all that through long ago. I told them everything, opening up my soul as if at confession. For an hour and a half I held forth, glancing only occasionally at my notes. In the beginning they tried to interrupt me, to ask questions, but then gave up. All I wanted was for them to hear me out, and then to close my eyes and listen to each of them in turn, then either to skulk off empty-handed, even more isolated than before, without hope or a vision, or else finally to have made sense of my life, in collective suicide in the name of freedom and liberation of the soul.

I understood only too well that attempting this change of attitude, this ethical perestroika, was not going to be a popular undertaking at a time when the whole thrust of society was towards getting kicks out of life, when powerful winds were fanning a forest fire in that one direction. I might find myself the only sacrifice in the cause of Sense, and that would render it pointless.

I buttressed my chosen position with the awareness that a great movement must plan only to gain the gratitude of future generations and should disregard the mood of the moment. This was a difficult time, but I was aware that these difficulties would pass and that our great movement, with its aspiration to renew the entire world, had no right to compromise with the mood of the moment but must look to the future.

I believe there is a law which means that the greater and more enduring its ultimate success in history, the less a movement will have been understood initially by the crowd, because its new propositions will have been directly contrary to the received wisdom of the masses, their desires and opinions. Accordingly, I never expected love, or even elementary understanding, from the broad masses. Today I had invited just four people who, I thought, might understand what I was getting at.

It was not the easiest of evenings! I was facing four people and had only a couple of hours in which to talk them round. Bit by bit I kicked away the foundations of their old way of seeing things. Bit by bit I overcame their resistance and gradually persuaded them. I had learned a new skill of taking the bull by the horns, foreseeing my opponent's objections and demolishing them in advance. I soon saw that my friends had recourse to a limited repertoire of objections and repeated the same arguments, and I was proud that I had means to counter all of them.

I remember thinking at the time that an orator reads on his audience's faces how well they are following what he says and the extent to which he is carrying them along with him. The audience spontaneously fine tunes what the speaker says. There is always a process of feedback between orator and audience. A speaker will frequently be confronted by prejudices derived solely from emotion rather than logic.

"Are you ready to give up your prejudices in order to move history in a fundamentally new direction?" I asked my listeners.

From the outset I had to cope with instinctive hostility, subconscious dislike, bias and negativity. It was much more difficult to combat these intuitive feelings than to overcome particular erroneous beliefs.

"Right, so what charge are we going to level at the current regime? Saparmurat Niyazov is dead, may he rest in peace. Dictatorship in Turkmenistan was consigned to oblivion along with him. What reason can we find for mounting an armed invasion?" Shargunov asked in puzzlement.

Having anticipated this objection, I now took from my file the speech which Kurbanbibi Atadjanova, the Public Prosecutor of Turkmenistan, had delivered on national television. It was called "An Attempt to Seize Power". I had been surprised to come across it on the way to this meeting, and it dealt with the unsuccessful bid to assassinate Niyazov and attempted coup d'etat in Turkmenistan on 25 November 2002. In an even, unhurried voice, I read them her indictment:

"We have indisputable evidence that the assassination attempt on the life of Turkmenbashi Saparmurat was instigated by Shikhmuradov, Hanamov, Yklymov, Orazov, Djumayev and their accomplices and that this was only the beginning of a chain of subsequent criminal acts which they were planning. While one group of terrorists was blocking the progress of the motorcade escorting the Sardar, others were biding their time in readiness to occupy the buildings of the Mejlis and national television.

"In order to perpetrate this exceptionally serious offence, the criminal, thief and terrorist Boris Shikhmuradov flew on 23 November to the Uzbek city of Karshi, then proceeded in a Volvo-840 to the central telephone office. On the same day around midnight, he illegally crossed the border and entered Turkmenistan.

"Early in the morning of 25 November 2002 Annamuradov Khatamov, being a member of a criminal association and Chief Engineer of the Turkmensuvdesga Institute, seated in his own vehicle in Archabil Avenue, observed President and Turmenbashi Saparmurat driving to work at his palace. As previously agreed, Khatamov then said over a portable radio to G. Djumayev the code words, "I'm on my way to work". At approximately 07.10 hrs, when President and Turkmenbashi Saparmurat was driving down Turkmenbashi Avenue and had passed the crossroads with Youth Street, Guvanch Djumayev drove a Kamaz truck on to Turkmenbashi Avenue, blocking the road to the escort vehicles of the Highway Supervisory Service. He leapt down from the cab and opened fire with an assault rifle.

"Simultaneously, individuals armed with assault rifles, five-chambered rifles, pistols, dressed in military fatigues and wearing black masks burst out of two Gazelle trucks concealed between buildings and a BMW parked on the opposite side of the street. Believing that the president was in one of the obstructed cars, they began firing from three directions with automatic rifles. In the course of this gunfire four soldiers of the Highway Supervisory Service were killed.

"In this way, B. Shikhmuradov intended to perpetrate an armed coup to change the system of government by force and in violation of the Constitution, to create an interim government with himself as its head, to take control of parliament and become president, undertaking to hold presidential elections within 24 months.

"In the course of the investigation, 51 weapons of various kinds (assault rifles, five-chambered rifles and pistols) were recovered from the criminals as material evidence and resources used to commit the crime.

"In the course of the investigation 46 dangerous criminals have been detained and arrested."

After reading all this out, I said, "Let me add that Boris Shikhmuradov received the maximum sentence of life imprisonment and there has been no information about his whereabouts for the past six years."

Fatigue suddenly overwhelmed me and I stopped. They too were silent. We sat there for a time at that wooden table, each with his own thoughts, a half-empty pot and cups still half-full of jasmine tea or already empty on the table in front of us. A gust of laughter came from a nearby table where a party of eight or nine people remembered something and laughed as one at the memory. Someone was smoking and dense clouds of cigarette smoke drifted through the subdued lighting in the basement where Sense was convening.

By now the four men knew all there was to know – about our standard, which was indeed a worthy symbol. We had before us a vivid icon of the ideals and aspirations of our new movement. They knew all about "Outlines of the Future State" and, to my surprise, approved of them warmly. They knew they would be required to change their entire lifestyle – I had read them "The Revolutionary's Catechism". They knew the invasion plan I had in mind. They knew that, in all probability, every man who flung himself into the abyss of this campaign would never get back out alive.

I saw no excitement in their eyes. Their faces too were calm. The battle which had taken place inside their hearts was over now and they seemed only to be waiting for me to raise my arm in the direction of the enemy and shout, "Attack!", but I too remained silent. Some distance away from our table, I saw a girl looking at me.

Her hair was as black as a moonless night, her eyes outlined in black, and even her lipstick was black. Barely noticeably, she smiled at me. She must have fancied me, but what use was that? If I stood up and hobbled over to her with my gammy leg disfigured by my destiny, just watch that smile change.

There was a hookah on her table and this girl, this 'warrior of the darkness' as I named her to myself, inhaled deeply. In the ball of smoke released from inside her, I saw images from the future.

I am in a black, military uniform with epaulettes and wearing a capacious black cap with a short peak. I am speaking from a podium and making frequent gestures. I open my mouth wide as I pronounce each word. I look like a man of power and substance.

"People do not understand that one who first demands of fate that it should guarantee success thereby renounces every vestige of heroism," I declare inexorably. "For heroism is precisely, in full awareness of imminent deadly danger, to take a bold step and thereby, just possibly, save the situation. If somebody has contracted cancer, he does not need to be 51 percent certain of a successful outcome before opting for surgery, because without it he will in any case die. If the operation holds out only one half of one percent of the prospect of recovery, the brave man will still choose to undergo the operation rather than merely snivel about his incurable illness. If we are at present living through a dispiriting phase of complete loss of willpower, of a complete loss of fortitude, this is most certainly the result of a fundamentally wrong approach in our country to the matter of upbringing. Dismaying consequences of this wrong approach to the upbringing of the young then inevitably have an adverse effect on every aspect of our lives and bring about a situation in which even the leaders of the state begin to suffer from a lack of civic courage."

People are hanging on my every word.

The girl takes another puff at her pipe and again

blows out hazy smoke in which I see my mother. She is very old now, withered and wizened, and she presses her ear to an old-fashioned wireless set from which my voice emerges. I know it is my voice even though I have never possessed such a voice. It is the voice of the future me, the voice of the man I aspire to become. Words stream invisibly into my mum's ear.

I am saying, "In the present-day social system everything is bogus, ridiculous – from religion which compels people to believe in that mirage of an overactive imagination, God, to the family, that social unit none of whose foundations stands up to even superficial examination; from the legalisation of commerce, which is mere organized thievery; from the acceptance as reasonable of a situation where the worker is worn down by toil, from which not he but the capitalist profits; to the position of women who are denied their political rights and set on a par with the animals.

"To escape from this fearful, oppressive situation, which is the ruin of modern man and in the struggle against which he fritters away most of his strength, we need revolution, revolution bloody and unsparing, revolution which will radically alter all, all without exception, foundations of modern society and destroy those who support the present system.

"We do not shy away from revolution, although we know that a river of blood will be shed and that there may also be innocent victims. We foresee all that, yet still we welcome its coming and are prepared to sacrifice our own lives to it.

"As for the present education system, as I said in one of our bulletins, it must be destroyed. Only on its ruins can we build our new meaningful society. Going to school and learning is nonsense because all educated people and the very act of becoming educated lead to exploitation. The developed inevitably exploit the less developed.

"To all of you listening to this speech in distant parts of the world, let me say that nothing can be absolutely correct and true. No view, no opinion is incontrovertibly superior to another, and which principle is loftier and more just than another is a matter only for the individual who adopts it or for those who share it. Protest against everything you find objectionable, because the sense of justice is still alive in many of you, and the best among you have not given up your desire to find the Sense in your existence. Follow our example: it is one of the destinies you can opt for. It is a destiny no worse and perhaps better than those the government, parents and universities propose. For centuries they have domesticated the most active of you and turned you into a docile herd.

"Students, for example, are active mainly during the first two years of colledge, but are then drawn into their studies, and by their fourth or fifth year have been completely tamed. When they graduate these rebels of yesteryear have been transformed into wholly reliable doctors, teachers, officials, family men and women and, when you look at some of them, it is difficult to believe that these are the same people who only three or four years ago spoke so fervently about the suffering of the common people and longed to sacrifice themselves for the common good. In no time at all, many become prosecutors, judges or investigators and join forces with the government to strangle the very people for whom only recently they believed and proclaimed they were willing to give their lives."

Tears flow from my mother's eyes. I know that, even though all I can see is the shuddering of her old grey head.

Then it all disappeared and I saw neither the girl at the far-off table with her hookah nor my comrades-in-arms.

Boris Shikhmuradov stood before me in front of the huge black banner of Sense with its red anemone inside a white circle. He recited to me the address to the peoples of the world which he wrote immediately before giving himself up to the Turkmen authorities.

"In recent days, the hunting for people and arrests have become increasingly repressive due to the fact that I am still at liberty. People are being beaten and subjected to psychological pressure in the most brutal manner solely in order to get them to admit that they have seen me somewhere or heard something about my whereabouts.

"I find it impossible to watch all this from the sidelines. In the hope that with my arrest the hounding of entirely innocent people will end, I have decided to voluntarily report to the Ministry of National Security of Turkmenistan.

"I assure all my supporters and others who think as I do that I will do my utmost to achieve the lofty goals we have set ourselves no matter what the cost: to rid Turkmenistan of Niyazov's dictatorship and hold free elections. Unfortunately, I have been unable to realize our main ideal while at liberty. It now remains for me to seek to do so while a captive of Niyazov. My immediate aim is to turn the trial of the democratic opposition into a trial of Niyazov's undemocratic regime.

"This present declaration I am making while still at liberty. Given the methods brought to bear on inmates of Niyazov's prisons, I can only speculate what awaits me in the near future. On more than one occasion we have seen how individuals have been manipulated not only by physical torture but also by barbaric methods of psychological pressure, making use of a variety of psychotropic drugs and other techniques to distort personality. I urge you to accept that I cannot be responsible for all my future statements which may be propagated by the media and law enforcement agencies under Niyazov's control.

"I have faith in the Turkmen people and their future in freedom."

After that, he looked me straight in the eye and said, "Artur Kara! I do not know where I am now or even whether I am alive, but here I can talk to you! Everybody has betrayed me, Artur! All my journalist friends have forgotten about me because they cannot think how to help. Russia, whose citizen I am, has sold me for gas. That's the truth! I was a token exchanged for a favourable gas price. They violated their own constitution by not demanding that I should be repatriated. They violated Russia's most fundamental statutes. While I was being tortured with electric shocks, beaten with clubs and all the rest of it, I clung to the hope, I believed that such international organisations as NATO and the UN, or those who support democratic values in Russia and claim to defend human rights, would save me from an unjust trial. But no, everyone just forgot me. Years passed, years, you know? I gave up hope.

"But I always knew, throughout my ordeal, that someone like you would appear and restore justice in this matter at least. I am so heartened that has finally come to pass.

"It doesn't matter whether you find me alive or dead in my solitary cell, or whether you find me at all. The banner of Sense in the sands of the Karakum Desert is already a liberation for me, a freeing of my soul."

"Artur! Artur!" I hear someone shouting near me. "Artur! What is wrong?" I hear someone else in a panic.

Boris gave me a wistful smile and waved. The dark banner of Sense billowed over him and he disappeared into its folds as if in a David Copperfield illusion. I was lying on a tiled floor and the faces of my supporters were looking down at me.

"Artur!" One of them gingerly patted me on the cheek. "You gave us a fright. Are you all right?"

My body was incredibly heavy and felt numb. Holding on to the hands of my people, I got up with difficulty and, as I looked round, remembered something.

"Do you know, my friends, Friedrich Nietzsche believed that mankind is a means, not an end in itself. Mankind is material for experimentation."

We talked on a little more and each of them promised to bring along a few reliable people. Some already had firearms, some had backers who would arrange for us to get into Turkmenistan. Soon everything would be resolved.

22

So then, my friends, I have written what I intended to write. I have revealed to you everything of value that I have in my heart after twenty years of living. I have told you what disturbs me, revealed my thoughts and hopes, and described where the thinking behind Sense came from that made me take up arms against the world.

The book you are about to finish reading has the lot. Here you have found youth, old age, generational conflict, and heroism. There has been a re-thinking of some of the fundamental truths of human life. The common thread running through my tale is death, which dogs me and informs every page of this tract.

I have never laid claim to any special destiny, but as things have turned out I am completely isolated and at odds with everyone around me. For all that, I still carry in my heart the remnants of a naive goodwill for which I have been unable to find a home. Everybody shunned me, until in the end I didn't care. I read a lot. That made me observant and I saw many things other people are blind to.

Tomorrow we are setting off for Turkmenistan. We have got together 136 fine soldiers, even more than I expected and all of them good, self-sacrificing men. Together with my action, this book will surely make my name and enable us to set Boris Shikhmuradov free, if it doesn't simply go unnoticed. Whatever, presumably, is the will of the Almighty.

Tomorrow at dawn I shall leave this manuscript at prearranged spot for someone I trust to collect. What he does with it is entirely up to him. He could have been with us but I have spared him. He may understand what I have to say better than others and may carry on our banner to future generations I will never see.

I am sitting here deep in thought and looking at our banner. "Anemone. Anemone. Anemone." I really like that name and the flower itself is beautiful. Delicate despite its toughness. *Anemos* is Greek for the wind.

> Here is a farewell poem.
> The end of life draws nigh
> And sparks of joy are far and few.
> Strange fate a river now run dry,
> No heavenly insights mine to view.
>
> I did not call but yet you came,
> Embraced me, left me in no doubt.
> I see you, Death, yet seek the fame
> And in my breast my heart cries out:

Wind, wind, blow today.
Let me fear no stormy weather.
Wind, wind, blow today.
Let us fly away together.
But when are you going to hear my plea?
Too soon a waning moon grows dim for me.

The path of life is at an end
But still there is a hope I cherish
That when I raise my eyes for one last prayer
I'll hear a caring voice before I perish.

Wind, wind, blow today.
Let me fear no stormy weather.
Wind, wind, blow today.
Let us fly away together.
But when are you going to hear my plea?
Too soon the waning moon grows dim for me.

Do not be sad. I will never leave you. I am the banner
of Sense. I look out from these lines. I am in the air you
breathe. I am you.

COMPLETE GLAS BACKLIST

Off the Beaten Track
Two Stories about Russian Hitchhiking

Mikhail Levitin, *A Jewish God in Paris*, three novellas

Roman Senchin, *Minus*, a novel
an old Siberian town surviving the perestroika dislocation

Maria Galina, *Iramifications*, a novel
adventures of today's Russian traders in the medieval East

Sea Stories. Army Stories
by **Alexander Pokrovsky** and **Alexander Terekhov**
realities of life inside the army

Andrei Sinyavsky, *Ivan the Fool: Russian Folk Belief*,
a cultural study

Sigizmund Krzhizhanovsky, *Seven Stories*
a rediscovered writer of genius from the 1920s

Leonid Latynin, *The Lair*,
a novel-parable, stories and poems

The Scared Generation,
two novels by **Vasil Bykov** and **Boris Yampolsky**
about persecution in Russia of the 1930s and '40s

Alan Cherchesov, *Requiem for the Living*, a novel,
the extraordinary adventures of an Ossetian boy set against
the traditional culture of the Caucasus

Nikolai Klimontovich, *The Road to Rome*,
naughty reminiscences about the late Soviet years

Nina Gabrielyan, *Master of the Grass*,
long and short stories by a leading feminist

Alexander Selin, *The New Romantic*, modern parables

Valery Ronshin, *Living a Life*, *Totally Absurd Tales*

Andrei Sergeev, *Stamp Album*, *A Collection of People,
Things, Relationships and Words*

Lev Rubinstein, *Here I Am*
humorous-philosophical performance poems and essays

Andrei Volos, *Hurramabad*,
national strife in Tajikstan following the collapse of the USSR

Larissa Miller, *Dim and Distant Days*
a Jewish childhood in postwar Moscow

Anatoly Mariengof, *A Novel Without Lies*
the turbulent life of a poet in flamboyant
Bohemian Moscow in the 1920s

Irina Muravyova, *The Nomadic Soul*,
a family saga about one more Anna Karenina

The Portable Platonov, a reader
for the centenary of Russia's greatest 20th century writer

Boris Slutsky, *Things That Happened*,
a biography of a major mid-20th century poet
interspersed with his poetry

Asar Eppel, *The Grassy Street*
graphic stories from a Moscow suburb in the 1940s

Peter Aleshkovsky, *Skunk: A Life*, a bildungsroman
set in the Northern Russian countryside

ANTHOLOGIES

Squaring the Circle,
winners of the Debut Prize for Fiction

War & Peace, army stories versus women's stories:
a compelling portrait of post-post-perestroika Russia

Strange Soviet Practices
short stories and documents illustrating
some inimitably Soviet phenomena

Captives
victors turn out to be captives on conquered territory

NINE of Russia's Foremost Women Writers
a collective portrait of women's writing today

Beyond the Looking-Glas, Russian grotesque revisited

A Will & a Way, women's writing of the 1990s

Childhood, the child is father to the man

Booker Winners & Others-II. The mid-1990s

Booker Winners & Others, mostly provincial writers

Love Russian Style, Russia tries decadence

Jews & Strangers, what it means to be a Jew in Russia

Bulgakov & Mandelstam, earlier autobiographical stories

Love and Fear, the two strongest emotions
dominating Russian life

Women's View, Russian women bloodied but unbowed

Soviet Grotesque,
young people's rebellion against the establishment

Revolution, the 1920s versus the 1980s

NON-FICTION

Michele A. Berdy, *The Russian Word's Worth*
A humorous and informative guide to
the Russian language, culture and translation

Contemporary Russian Fiction: A Short List
11 Russian authors interviewed by Kristina Rotkirch

**Nina Lugovskaya, *The Diary of a Soviet Schoolgirl:
1932-1937***, the diary of a Russian Anne Frank

Alexander Genis, *Red Bread*, essays
Russian and American civilizations compared
by one of Russia's foremost essayists

A.J. Perry, *Twelve Stories of Russia: A Novel, I guess*